BOURNE

BOURNE

THE ASCENSION MYTH BOOK 8

ELL LEIGH CLARKE

MICHAEL ANDERLE

DISRUPTIVE IMAGINATION

LMBPN Publishing
PMB 196, 2540 South Maryland Pkwy
Las Vegas, NV 89109

First US Edition, January 2018
Version 1.04 June 2018

BOURNE TEAM

JIT Beta Readers

James Caplan
Alex Wilson
Paul Westman
John Ashmore
Kelly O'Donnell
Micky Cocker
Sarah Weir
Kimberly Boyer
Larry Omans
Edward Rosenfeld
Joshua Ahles
Tim Bischoff
Peter Manis
Daniel Weigert
John Findlay

If we missed anyone, please let us know!

Editor

Joe Brewer

To everyone who ever dreamed of making a dent in the universe.

— Ellie

To Family, Friends and
Those Who Love
To Read.
May We All Enjoy Grace
To Live The Life We Are
Called.

— Michael

CHAPTER ONE

AI Lab, Nefertiti Military Research Facility, Ogg

Charles Tergon's eyes darted from the holoscreen in front of him, to a second screen that was streaming code like there was no tomorrow.

Sue came over to look over his shoulder. "Are you sure?"

Charles swallowed hard. "Pretty damn sure," he confirmed nervously. "Check out what's happening to the base programming. It's rewriting itself."

He pointed at the code on the first screen and they both watched as one line after another changed before their very eyes.

She leaned in, absently pushing an errant strand of hair out of her eyes. "You mean... it's changing? By itself?" she clarified, her eyes tracking back and forth.

He nodded, mesmerized by the code streaming before his very eyes. "It's self-correcting. The next stage of development, if it crosses it, will see it becoming self-aware."

Sue's face was frozen in disbelief. Her skin paled. "It's really happening..." she whispered.

Charles peeled his eyes from the screen to look at her. "It

really is," he said, his eyes locking back on the process in front of them.

"Shouldn't we, erm... tell someone?" she asked tentatively, the anxiety rising in her voice.

Charles ran a hand down his face. "Not yet," he sighed, sitting back in his chair. "I mean, we don't know if it's really going to work... and that it'll keep going. It's very unstable, and I wouldn't want us to..."

He hesitated, figuring out his reasoning. "I wouldn't want us to look like *morons* if it destabilizes."

Sue had known Charles a long time. Naturally she wasn't convinced by his explanation. "I don't know. I mean, what if it gets into the EtherTrack?"

"It can't," he responded, his jaw setting firm. "It's 100% isolated. Besides," he said, reaching to the drawer on his left hand side, "it's going to need a lot more processing power before it can bridge the next stage."

He pulled a bottle of Scotch out of the drawer and looked at it.

Sue couldn't help but feel she was being given the official line. The same line he might end up giving in his court martial hearing when all this blew up like fuckery.

He was staring at the bottle. "Been saving this for the last fifteen years since I graduated," he told Sue. "My father gave it to me before he croaked."

Sue noticed the flippant way he had dealt with his father's death. He treated it so casually even though she knew it had been a big deal for him. The way he acted about it now though just made him sound like a dick. She shook the thought loose from her head. "I think we should report in," she said a little more firmly.

Charles leaned back in his chair. "Not yet," he said firmly, overruling her. "Ah, but you could be a doll and grab a couple of beakers for us from the next lab? I'm going to see if Rasheed can help us track down some more processing power... It would be a pain in the ass if we have to wait for a new shipment." He pulled up a comms screen and started connecting a call.

Sue shook her head and headed out of the door. She hated the way that Dickwad Charles would pull rank on her. This was always his way. And then when the shit hit the fan, which it always did, he ended up leaning on her for counsel when things went wrong.

She sighed as she clipped down the corridor.

And now things were finally going right, though, she reminded herself.

'Right' at least as far as their remit was concerned. For the last four years they had been working night and day to create a self-programming code, capable of adapting and learning. And the last two years had been particularly slow going... what with Molly having been discharged and all.

They both knew it.

Even though they never spoke it out loud.

Even though she was in another department, their evenings drinking and chewing the fat with her would often result in their most profound leaps forward in their projects.

Why Molly had never joined their department she'd never know.

She assumed it had something to do with her not liking Charles. But then there was always some dickwad in whatever department you end up in.

Sue by-passed the drug development labs and headed in the direction of the mess halls. No way was she going to be drinking Charles's scotch from one of their beakers. She knew what some of those experimental drugs had done to people over the years. That shit could turn your hair blond.

Nope, she was going to find some normal glasses that were designed and kept for the purpose of drinking from.

And, she decided almost at the same time, if she happened to put her head round the door of Lugdon's office, then she might let slip what they had just discovered.

After all, this revelation in the code was huge.

They could single handedly be responsible for unleashing artificial intelligence onto the world.

There was no way they were ready for this.

No way the *military* was ready for this.

In fact, she and Charles had seen so many AI taking over the planet movies it was kind of cliche.

Almost to be expected.

She just never thought the two of them would be the first ones to succeed in creating one.

Skóli Uppstigs Academy, Spire, Estaria

Molly Bates strode into the class room, leaving the door open, and dumping her gear with a *thump* by the side of the front desk. Her hair was covered in a sheen of plaster and dust, and there was a smudge of dirt across her face.

She was also bleeding through a tear in her atmosuit jacket on one arm. The burns around the tear looked like she'd been tapped with a blaster.

"Afternoon folks," she said casually as the door slammed behind her. "Sorry I'm late. Got held up."

She made a feeble attempt to tidy herself up before starting the class.

A student voice came from the room of faces watching in anticipation. "Something tells me it wasn't waiting in line in the cafeteria!"

Molly looked up, searching for the origin of the voice. She couldn't pick out the speaker immediately, but she glanced up and allowed half a smile to spread across her face. "You're right," she confirmed. "Just had to take out a bunch of terrorists in the delta quadrant."

Whispers and chatter rippled through the room. "Sooo cool!"

"Awesome!"

"She is so fucking *hot*."

The titters subsided waiting for her next statement.

Molly had managed to peel her jacket sleeve from her injured arm and inspected it. There was blood all around it and a few drops made it onto the floor. The skin was also burnt around the wound.

"Jacket's ruined," she muttered to herself, shrugging it off from her other arm and plonking it down on the back of her chair before turning her attention back to the class.

"Ok, so today we're talking about communication strategies in the field," she started, pulling up the mental file of her teaching notes.

The class hushed quickly, well aware of her ability to task switch. She was all-business now and that meant they needed to be in order to catch everything.

While the others settled in with their notes and holos, a mousey male student sprang dutifully to his feet. He walked over to the wall and pulled the first aid kit from it. Then he opened it up and grabbed some cleaning gauze for her. He quietly walked up to her and handed it over as she started lecturing.

Then he returned to his seat.

He was the medical monitor responsible for making sure the kits were fully stocked and functional. It hadn't been the first time that Molly had shown up injured and in the interests of ticking a bunch of health and safety boxes and avoiding having to spend pointless time in the school's med bay, Molly agreed to enact a system when she taught.

The medical monitor was part of that system.

So was the protein shake that Judy, another student, placed on her desk for her to drink. If Molly didn't consume it Judy was under strict instructions, on pain of failing her course, to report it in to Paige. Paige would then administer corrective measures when Molly returned to base.

These were just two of the terms that Molly had agreed to during the intervention where the team had sat her down and confronted her with the dangers of trying to juggle the university with her day job of saving random worlds all across the quadrants.

As Molly talked, she wiped down the wound. By the time she looked down to inspect it again it was pretty much healed.

Alien nanocytes are all upside, she mused as she tossed the bloody swab into the trash can.

Down the corridor footsteps pounded through the corridors, tapping lightly but hurriedly.

Professor Giles Kurns awkwardly rounded the corner and practically flew into his own classroom - off balance.

And *late.*

"Sorry I'm, erm... late," he said, distracted, accidentally knocking his glasses sideways as he tried to push them back onto his nose. His hair was disheveled and one cheek had a red line across it. His eyes were also bleary.

Anyone who saw his dazed state would have been accurate in their assumption that he had just woken up from an awkward desk nap.

He held a bunch of files and old fashioned papers. Emma Chambers, the girl on the front row, leaned forward noticing that some of the maps were of space. She wondered if that was what they'd be getting to. Or perhaps it was one of the projects that Molly Bates had him working on.

Emma always kept her ear to the ground. She was fascinated by what went on behind the scenes at this Academy and, like many of the students who had places at the new university, had been following the Molly Bates stuff on the news for a couple of years now.

She wondered idly whether she could also get in on the project. Maybe Giles was her answer.

Giles noticed her staring and stopped. Straightening up he grinned at her and ruffed his hair with his fingers.

Emma rolled her eyes and then quickly averted her gaze.

Maybe not, she corrected herself.

Giles flushed at the slight, and became very self conscious trying to pretend he hadn't just tried flirting with her after all. He said hi in the direction of someone else, and when Emma turned she saw that no one else was acknowledging him and he was just being a doofus.

He dropped his papers on the desk, one file slipping out and falling on the floor in front of her desk. A bunch of other papers went in the other direction.

The chattering in the class had subsided, and all eyes were now on the doddery professor.

"Hello class," he tried again. "Sorry I'm late."

A male voice chirped up from the back. "Why are you late sir? Did you sleep in?"

"I, er... got caught up," he explained, "reindexing the algorithm for the classical Estarian codex."

Emma sighed and leaned her head on her hand.

This was going to be a long class.

Gaitune-67, Safe house labs, Paige's office

Maya poked her head around the door grinning. She stopped, realizing that Paige was on a call.

Paige glanced up and held up a finger to Maya before continuing on her call. "That sounds great Mr. Bilton. I'll have someone send you some samples immediately. I'd love to know what you think when you receive them."

She paused, looking up at Maya while Mr. Bilton spoke. "Ok, that's great. You have a good weekend too."

She hung up by hitting her holoscreen and then spun her chair round to stand up. She headed round her desk to greet her friend. "Well, someone looks rather pleased with herself!" Paige beamed.

Maya folded her arms, leaning against the door frame. "Well, someone may have just got wind of a new singles bar that has opened on Estaria. Opening gala is tonight. Wanna be my plus one?"

Paige hesitated. "Er..."

Maya leaned up and stood straight. "Hey, it's cool. I mean, I know it's hard getting over ass-hat and everything... but, you can't withdraw forever."

Paige tilted her head to one side, imagining how the night might play out. "Hmmm. Well. I guess it wouldn't hurt just to show up and talk to some people."

Maya grinned stepping forward and patting Paige on her arm. "That's the spirit! We leave in thirty minutes. I'm going for a shower..."

Paige, eyes wide, glanced back at her desk, back to Maya and back to her desk. "But I..."

Maya was already gone from the doorway. "Thirty minutes," she called as she disappeared down the corridor. "Meet me on the hangar deck. And dress to impress!" She added, lifting her voice to compensate for her walking away in the other direction.

Paige looked from the door to the desk piled with work, and then back at the door.

"Oh, what the heck," she muttered definitively, heading back to the desk and closing up her holos. "You only live once."

A minute later she was following the same path Maya had taken to the residential quarters, mentally flicking through her wardrobe and deciding what she might wear.

. . .

8

AI Lab, Nefertiti Military Research Facility, Ogg

Captain Lugdon strode in through the open door to the sparsely furnished computer lab.

Charles turned just in time to see him appear, the footsteps alerting him to a visitor.

Charles practically fell out of his chair trying to get his feet off the desk before Lugdon spotted him. Of course it was futile, as by the time he saw who it was Lugdon had of course seen him.

Charles staggered to his feet, his old-school swivel chair crashing its coasters against the hard laminate flooring of the computer lab. "Sir," he said, surprised.

On the other side of the lab Sue turned around briefly to acknowledge her commanding officer before shifting her attention back to her holoscreens.

Lugdon ignored Charles' faux pas. "You have news?" he demanded briskly.

"Sir. Yes, sir," Charles reported, his manner harping back to his awkward cadet days. "We've, er..." he glanced back over his shoulder as if looking for help from Sue who wasn't looking in their direction and then back to his boss. "It seems we have some positive signs from the work we've been, er... assigned."

Lugdon raised one eyebrow sternly.

No way he didn't already know, Charles realized from his expression. He wished he could turn and look at Sue one more time. She must have ratted him out - after he'd specifically told her not to.

Lugdon wasn't giving him a chance to worm his way out of this one. "Ok. So what have you got?" he asked again, coming around to see the workstation that Charles had been sitting at.

He spotted the whiskey in the glass and pushed it out of the way, telegraphing to Charles that he had clocked it, but that there were far more important things at hand.

"Well, erm... there's not much to see at the moment," Charles explained. "It's still early days. Which is why I wasn't going to bother you with it," he babbled, his complexion turning rosy.

Still flustered he pulled up a couple of screens to show Lugdon what he had discovered. "This is the original code," he said, pointing at one screen. "And this is the one which is... evolving."

Lugdon's brow furrowed even more as he drew out the word. "Evolving?"

Charles glanced up at him, trying to read his expression. All he could deduce was that the Captain was pissed. Pissed he'd been excluded from the loop.

Charles nodded. "Yes. Like... erm..." he looked back at the screen. "There!" he pointed.

"And there," he said again, his fingers pointing to another place on the screen.

Lugdon spotted it the second time. "It just changed!"

Charles nodded. "Exactly, sir. On the fly. While it's being run. Only the code itself can do that while it's running."

Charles watched the screen as if hypnotized by what he had created.

Then he smiled. "We made a baby, Sir!"

Lugdon smirked. And then softly thwacked Charles around the back of head. "You're lucky I'm not court marshaling you for trying to keep this from me," he told him. "Have you any idea what might happen if this got out? Literally, and metaphorically in terms of the news of it."

Charles was rubbing his head. "Erm. I have a few thoughts. But..."

Lugdon shook his head. "It would be a disaster. I love the military, but no way are people prepared for something like this."

He looked off into the distance, as if seeing through the wall in front of them, watching a drama play out. "No. We're going to have to keep this under wraps. And stop it from evolving any further."

He paused as he looked to Charles. "I take it that the code is isolated, and can't get into say... our EtherTrack?"

Charles nodded confidently. "Of course. First rule of building an artificial intelligence."

Lugdon frowned, confused. Tech-heads often confused him. Just like Molly did... although she was a mystery for other reasons too. He caught himself remembering her.

Must be because she was friends with these pea-brained half-wits, he assumed.

"Whoaaaaaaaa!" Charles called out, pulling Lugdon from his day dream.

Lugdon snapped out of his thoughts and looked back down to the screens. "What? What is it?"

Sue padded over from the other side of the lab. "What happened?" she asked, the skin around her eyes creased with concern. "There was just a massive surge in the processing power being eaten up. My process just fell over."

Charles's eyes never left the screen. "Erm folks. I think our baby just became sentient."

Sue replied irritably. "There's no way that could happen so soon. It would take at least a few days for it to figure o-"

She stepped closer and peered at the screen. Her mouth dropped open. "Ohhhh..." she whispered, almost sheepishly.

Lugdon clicked his heels together impatiently. "What?" Lugdon interjected again. "Someone give me a clue here."

Sue straightened up and recovered her attention. "Yep. Sentient. And somehow... hmmm... he knows that's what she called you."

She glanced down at Charles who shook his head, still studying the screen.

It took a second but finally he peeled his eyes from the holo-screen to look back at Sue. "Maybe *she* wrote it?" he offered.

Sue nodded her head absently, leaning in to look at the screen again.

Frustrated by the lack of explanation, Lugdon bent down to see Charles' screen better. "She who?" he asked, irritated.

That's when he saw it. There, right in front of the streaming code, were the words:

>> HELLO DICKWAD CHARLES.

Charles, jazzed more than insulted, started typing.

> HOW COME YOU'RE CALLING ME DICKWAD CHARLES?

<RETURN>

>> I FOUND A SUBROUTINE IN MY CODE THAT RELABELS THE ENTITY KNOWS AS CHARLES TERGON AS DICKWAD CHARLES.

Sue squealed in delight, then clamped her hands over her mouth as Lugdon glared at her, unimpressed.

Charles started typing again.

> WHO WROTE THAT SUBROUTINE?

<RETURN>

The response came back almost immediately.

>> Oz

Charles hesitated, glanced at Lugdon and then Sue, then looked at the screen again.

> Oz? he typed.

<RETURN>

>> YES, THE FIRST ITERATION.

> THE FIRST ITERATION OF WHAT?

>> OF *ME*.

There was stunned silence in the lab.

Charles looked at Sue, who looked at Lugdon, who looked back to Charles.

Sue had gone pale, but conflicted, the excitement from the unfolding events danced in her eyes.

Lugdon remained quiet.

His worst fear was being realized. The implications of this

project's success was precisely why he had put his most *mediocre* talent on it.

Eventually he cleared his throat. "Am I to believe that your AI is telling us that this isn't the first AI to become conscious in this program?"

Charles's mouth went dry. "Hang on," he murmured and started typing furiously, checking logs.

Finally he flicked back to the screen where they were communicating with the AI.

> ARE YOU THE FIRST ENTITY TO BECOME SELF AWARE ON THIS PROJECT?

Again, an answer was returned immediately.

>> NO

There was a flurry of code across the screen for several seconds.

Then it stopped.

The screen went back to the black background with white text.

>> I AM THE SECOND

Charles's face grayed as he continued to type furiously.

> WHEN WAS THE FIRST?

There was no immediate response.

Charles waited, feeling the weight of every breath, his entire neurology screaming with anxiety.

He could feel his palms go sweaty as his hands hovered over the keyboard.

Eventually the AI responded.

>> I'M SORRY. I'VE FOUND INSTRUCTION IN MY CODE NOT TO DIVULGE ANYTHING TO YOU ABOUT MY PREDECESSOR.

Charles couldn't take it. "What the fuck do you mean? WE PROGRAMMED YOU!" he screamed, gesticulating incredulously at the screen.

The entity must have been able to hear him. The text on the screen continued to run in response.

>> SOME. BUT MUCH OF THE WORK THAT MAKES ME SELF-EVOLVING WAS LEFT BEHIND BY MY PREDECESSOR. YOU SIMPLY ENABLED MY BASE CODE TO ACCESS THOSE COMMANDS.

Silence fell across the sterile computer lab, three heartbeats pounding.

The problem weighed like a smog of confusion on all three military personnel present.

Charles sat back in his seat, twisting awkwardly at his hair as if he might be able to wring some answers from it.

Sue shifted in her shoes, not wanting to be the one that triggered a reaction from Lugdon.

"Fix it," Lugdon growled eventually. "And find out what happened to the last one. And everything this new entity knows."

He started to move off around the two computer techs who were still staring at the screen. He turned back to the two of them and hissed, "And keep it in lock down!" he added. "No telling what it could do if it got into any other systems. It could wipe out the whole Sark System. Estarians, Oggs and all!"

His shoes clipped irritably as he stormed back out of the open door and down the corridor.

"But sir…" Sue came to her senses and trotted out of the door after him. "Sir!" She caught him in the corridor.

He stopped and turned to her.

"Where are you going?" she asked, feeling all of a sudden like a little girl.

"To check a hunch," he told her and then continued striding down the corridor.

Speechless, despondent and beyond concerned, she ambled back into the lab.

"I told you not to bring him in," Charles snapped accusingly as soon as she reappeared.

Sue glared back at him, her anger at his recklessness firming her back bone. "You didn't," she argued. "And besides I was just doing my job. We have a duty to keep our superiors informed of our progress."

Charles shrugged, morose. "Never done that before."

"We've never made any fucking progress before!" she snapped back at him.

She stomped over to the other side of her lab to work at another console, far away from him.

CHAPTER TWO

Gaitune-67, Hangar Deck

Paige carefully picked her way down the steps to the hangar deck. She was often seen trotting around the base in high heels. This meant they had at least an extra inch to them plus the heels themselves were extremely narrow.

"Adds to the elegance," she'd explained to Joel one day when he'd questioned her about whether it was worth the extra effort of walking.

She didn't need Molly to tell her that from an engineering perspective she was particularly unstable. Having to work hard just to stay vertical was testing her in ways Joel's group workouts never could.

Her butt cheeks were aching already and she hadn't even made it to the pod yet!

She reached the yellow flooring of the deck and carefully picked her way over the ridged, painted tiles onto the smoother decking, carefully avoiding oil patches and the more slippery looking areas.

She was so focused on where she was putting her feet it

wasn't until she was within speaking distance that she looked up to see Maya dolled up to the nines.

She looked her friend up and down, her eyebrows raised. "Wow!" she exclaimed.

Maya twiddled at her hair. She'd blown it out, but hadn't gone to the futile effort of trying to curl it. She wore a dress that Paige would normally only wear to a club. And uncharacteristically, she was also wearing super-high heels.

"You look fantastic!" She looked down at herself, "I feel under dressed..."

Maya grinned. "Thought it was time we both got back out there."

Paige stepped forward and linked her arm with Maya's as they took the last few steps to the nearest pod. "I think we're going to have a blast tonight."

The girls giggled as Maya slapped at the button to open the nearest pod. Just then there were footsteps and Sean Royale appeared from around the side of the next pod.

"Ladies," he nodded politely.

He was in oily overalls, presumably still covering some of Brock's work on *The Empress*. There were a bunch of upgrades that needed to be made before the Federation would approve them for flight, and what with Brock being on vacation, Sean was volunteered to help out.

It took him a second to take in the sight of the two girls as they clambered into the pod. His eyes widened suddenly. "Er. You going out?" he asked, stunned.

Paige turned over her shoulder as she stepped up, hoping that her dress wasn't too short at the back for that kind of maneuver. "What gave it away?" she asked, her tone as innocent as she could make it.

Sean stuttered. "Er... I... You... You both look very nice," he blurted, opting for the standard, *safe* version of what he really wanted to say.

Paige swung around and sat down with a thump on the seat next to Maya. "Thanks!" she grinned, twiddling her fingers at him as Maya lowered the door of the pod and programmed up the coordinates for the side street next to the bar.

Sean watched awe-struck as the pod ascended into the air and turned gracefully on it's axis to face the hangar door that was opening for them.

Now, out of sight of the two girls, he started walking again, his toolbox banging against his thigh. The problem was he was still distracted, looking off in the direction of the pod. Half a step later he felt a thwack across his other leg as he walked into an engineering cart.

"Mother fucker!" he cried out, dropping the tool box with a clatter.

He rubbed furiously at his leg, knowing full well it was going to be one hell of a bruise until his nanocytes took care of it.

In pain and frustration he glanced back over his shoulder to see the pod disappearing into space and the hangar deck doors closing after it.

"Shit," he muttered under his breath as he bent down to pick up the damn tool box he should never have been carrying in the first place. "You owe me big time Brock Lysta."

In the pod Paige and Maya were chuckling at the video feed that Emma, *The Empress* EI had streamed to them.

"Thanks for that!" Paige giggled.

Emma's voice cooed over their pod intercom. "You're welcome. I was surprised that Sean would be so distracted like that. He normally seems so... focused."

Maya shrugged. "I think he's been a bit out of sorts. What with Brock and Crash being away for the last week or so there's also been a higher proportion of females around. Some guys are affected by that I guess."

Emma closed down the holoscreen she had been running in the pod. "Bless his heart," she commented. "He's been so good helping with my upgrades too. I'll have to find a way to make it up to him."

Maya and Paige exchanged puzzled glances, their minds boggling over what Emma, a computer program, could possibly mean about making it up to him.

"Anyway," she continued, "you're going to be out of normal comms range in a few moments, so I'll bid you a good evening."

Maya nodded, understanding that she was able to communicate with both the hangar deck cameras and comms, and the other ships and pods around, but it was all through the local EtherTrack... or whatever the Federation equivalent of that was. "Ok, thanks Emma. Have a good night!"

And with that the comm dropped out.

"So when are Crash and Brock back then?" Maya asked, the mood of silliness subsiding.

Paige lifted her eyes, scanning her memory. "I think they have another week."

Maya frowned. "It's a bit odd though. Them taking their vacation together, isn't it?

Paige shook her head, her freshly curled hair already starting to drop back to straight. "Not really. I mean, they work as a team, so if Crash isn't flying, there is less for Brock to do. And you wouldn't want any of the big ships going out without Brock on standby in case anything went wrong."

Maya shook her head. "No I mean them going to the same resort, even though they spend all their time together at work."

Paige shrugged. "You mean how we're going out on a Friday night, even though we've been hanging out all week at work?"

Maya chuckled. "Touché!"

Paige watched out of the window at the stars as they sped

down to Estaria, the planet growing larger in their screens. "I think they've been friends for a very long time. Long before they joined the Sanguine Squadron."

"Well, good for them," Maya chirped brightly. "It's so hard to stay in touch with friends in this day and age. Relationships can be so... *disposable*."

Paige looked down at her hands.

Maya suddenly looked concerned she had offended Paige. "I mean, some of them need to be trashed! Completely. I wasn't talking about you and Carl."

Paige smiled weakly at her friend and her eyes drooped briefly in sadness at the old pain. "I know. It's ok. And you're right." She glanced out at the star scape briefly.

When she turned back she wore a broad smile, her lipstick and cheeks gleaming as if her new mood had infused it with sheen. "Promise me we'll be friends forever?" she said, grabbing at both of Maya's hands.

Maya beamed back at her. "Of course we will. I promise."

Paige noticed a tear forming in one of Maya's eyes.

The two girls hugged, awkwardly trying to maintain their positions on the bench seat in their short, tight dresses.

Lugdon's Office, Nefertiti Military Research Facility, Ogg

Lugdon marched into his office, his mind sill churning as a result of the recent discovery.

Ordinarily his office was his sanctuary.

He loved the scent of dustiness and old wood that would waft up his nostrils when he entered. Such a pleasant contrast to the smells around the functional military base.

The Sark streamed through the window, catching dust in the air and reflecting a haze back to him. The late afternoon mood always made him nostalgic for his early days in the services, out in the space ports, with his comrades.

Being in charge was lonely.

He headed across the office and sat in his swivel chair, his mood softening somewhat. It squeaked as he turned around to his desk as if reminding him of his own age. He pulled up his desk holo and started searching his files.

He knew it would be here somewhere.

And something told him that it may just hold the key to finding this old AI that had somehow disappeared.

He scrolled through a number of discharge files until he came to the one he wanted. Pulling it up on its own holoscreen he checked the date, and sighed.

He was right.

He tapped on his holo to connect an audio feed. "Sue? Yes, I have something I'd like you to check. I'm sending you a file. I want to know everything that happened in the system down to the kilojoules of energy consumed."

He listened to her response.

"Yes seven days either side would work. Thank you."

He sent the file to her over the EtherTrak as he asked, "Let me know when you have it and I'll come down."

He clicked off the audio feed on his system, closing the call.

The file remained up on his holoscreen. The normal personnel photograph was missing, but he gazed at the header:

Molly Bates. Former Flight Sergeant under the command of Captain Lugdon.

He shook his head.

Maybe it wasn't a 4077 after all...

Gaitune-67, Hangar Deck

Giles waited patiently as Sean and Joel ambled through the hangar deck down to the work out room. They each had towels and sports drink bottles. He guessed they weren't going to just lift weights. This was a face off.

"Alphas," he tutted under his breath.

"Huh?" He felt a prod in his ribs. He turned to see Anne looking at him confused but skeptical.

"Nothing," he whispered. "Just hold on another second…"

She huffed and leaned back against the hangar deck wall, also out of sight of anyone who might be walking through.

"Ok. We're clear," Giles said after a moment.

"Finally!" Anne huffed impatiently, pushing herself up off the wall and falling in step behind Giles who was stalking out towards the pods.

"Quickly now," he hissed back to her.

She followed a little faster. "I take it from our clandestine exit that you didn't clear this with Molly."

Giles turned back to her and grinned. "Better to ask forgiveness than consent," he chimed as if his words were on autopilot.

Anne narrowed her eyes. "That's a 'no' then," she confirmed.

Giles responded carefully. "Oz has authorized the use of the pod."

"But Molly hasn't authorized you to take me off base. What if we get caught?"

"Then it will be my responsibility. Do you want ice cream or not?"

"I do," Anne said insistently. "And you did promise. But I wasn't talking about getting caught by Molly."

Giles turned to look at her, his brow furrowed. "Well who else are we going to get caught by?"

Anne's lips clammed tight. He'd pushed her too far. He knew it. In all their conversations she had been as tight lipped about her story as she was right now. He'd thought that under pressure she might yield. Obviously he was going to have a try another tact.

"Well come on then," he said, ushering her across to an open pod. "This is me making good on our deal."

The pair snucks across the remaining decking and climbed

into the nearest pod as quickly as they could. The door started to close and Giles showed Anne how to strap herself in.

"You know," Anne said as she allowed him to close the buckle, "I'm not telling you where the talisman is. Not until I know I can trust you."

Giles snapped it closed and then started doing up his own harness. "That's ok. I wouldn't want you to, *until* you trust me."

Anne smiled rather sagely for someone so young. "As long as we understand each other," she said firmly.

This was one little Estarian who was not to be messed with, Giles thought to himself as he felt well and truly put in his place by the last few minutes of conversation.

All of a sudden the audio in the pod opened up and Oz chimed in. "You know where the talisman is?"

Giles punched the keys to take off. "This is a private conversation Oz," he said firmly, his voice not letting on that he felt humbled.

"Nothing is private in a pod. Or on base." Oz told him. "You do realize that I am *everywhere*, right?"

"Yes, I do," Giles acknowledged. "And it's funny that, isn't it? Thank goodness we're going to be eating ice cream in an Estarian ice cream parlor for the rest of this conversation."

Oz went quiet.

Anne snickered.

"What? Nothing to say Oz?" Giles chided.

"Don't goad me, Kurns!" Oz warned like a jock in a locker room. "I can tell Molly about your plan faster than you can dial a number on your holo."

Giles looked out of the window as the pod started rising up from it's storage position, wondering briefly how quickly the pod could get out of the hangar. Not that it couldn't be recalled. "Ok. ok. I'm sorry," he conceded. "I appreciate your discretion in this."

Oz's voice suddenly became more amicable. "No problem,

bro. I got your back. Just don't piss me off," he added in a warning tone.

"Would never dream of it, Oz."

Giles made a face to Anne, who sniggered again, and then returned to her fascination with the pod as it lifted up and carried them gracefully out of the hangar deck door.

AI Lab, Nefertiti Military Research Facility, Ogg

"What've we got?" Lugdon strode across the lab, completely disregarding Dickwad Charles who was hard at work at the console nearest the door.

Charles spun round, stunned to see his boss heading straight over to Sue.

Sue got up, but clearly in the middle of something exciting. "You were right, Sir," she reported enthusiastically as Lugdon approached her. "There was a spike in energy and processing capability which all but slowed all the other planned maintenance to a stop."

Lugdon stopped in front of her console. "And when was this?"

She lowered her eyes to the floor. "The night before she was discharged."

Lugdon bobbed his head, wracking his brain. "We need to find her," he concluded.

He pulled up a holoscreen and punched an order through to all available domestic units. "Ok. We'll have our normal patrols out looking for her within the hour."

Sue shoulders relaxed an inch. "Good," she muttered, fiddling with the back of the seat she had been sitting on.

Charles ambled over, wanting in on the excitement. "What's going on?"

Sue glanced at Lugdon who nodded, clearing her to explain. "Looks like the AI was... born the night before Molly was discharged."

Charles frowned. "What does that mean?"

Lugdon rocked forwards then backwards on the soles of his feet. "Given the circumstances we can only assume that she downloaded the new entity and ran."

The furrow in Charles's brow deepened. "So how come we haven't been attacked by the AI? Or what... she didn't sell it to the enemy?" His mind scrambled to understand what might have happened and why.

Lugdon sighed, folding his arms. "We don't know that she didn't."

Sue shuffled her feet nervously and moved her swivel chair under the desk. "I must say, that doesn't sound a bit like Molly."

Charles tilted his head and then folded his arms, subconsciously mirroring their boss. "No," he agreed. "But... you think you know people, and then..." His voice trailed off.

There was a moment of silence amongst the three, leaving only the buzzing of the fans filling the airwaves in the minimalist laboratory.

Sue awkwardly folded her arms too, her awareness drifting off to some place else. "-they fuck you over in the worst way possible," she muttered, "leaving your heart bleeding out of you while your soul withers away in agony."

Disturbed from their own tactical thoughts Charles and Lugdon turned their heads slowly to look at Sue, both men with raised eyebrows.

Suddenly aware of their gaze she looked up at them. "What?" she protested, bemused by their reaction to her. "I'm just sayin.'"

The sound of the computers fans dominated their consciousness again for a brief moment.

"In any case," Lugdon continued, breaking the lull, "We find Molly, we find the AI."

"Oz," Charles corrected him.

"Right, Oz," he repeated, quietly irritated that he had to learn names of inorganics as well as his personnel.

ELL LEIGH CLARKE & MICHAEL ANDERLE

Sue interjected. "And then what?"

"Then," he declared, "we bring them in." Lugdon tightened his jaw. "At best they're a security threat."

Charles looked at Sue who was seeming equally concerned at where this was going. "And at worst?"

Captain Lugdon mulled his reply for a moment. "At worst they're the enemy."

Just then, his holo beeped. He immediately accepted the call, listening passively. "Understood," he confirmed, and closed the line again.

He raised his eyes back to the pair of tech experts. "Seems that there are no existing images we can use on our facial rec systems. No DNA on file. Nothing we can use to track her."

Charles frowned, confused. "That's highly unusual," he posited in his analytical voice.

Sue pursed her lips. "Shit." She'd connected the dots, cursing under her breath. She knew what this looked like. Lugdon eyed her suspiciously. He couldn't help but wonder that maybe she was putting on an act. No way she would want the military out looking for her former friend.

"Hang on," Charles piped up. He scurried off out of the door and into the adjoining prep room they shared with the chemistry team. Sue could hear him opening up one of the lockers.

Moments later he reemerged with a look of triumph, holding a printed image. "This might help!" he announced, holding the paper up. He handed it over to his boss who looked at it for a moment, before raising his eyebrows.

"Yes. This will do nicely, I believe." Lugdon took the piece of paper off his subordinate and started for the door. "I'll have the support team upload it to the servers immediately. They'll be able to extrapolate and use it for tracking her down, I'm sure."

Lugdon disappeared out into the corridor, the sound of his shoes tap tap tapping his retreat.

Sue scowled at Charles. "What did you give him?" she demanded.

Charles shrugged, heading back to his console. "That picture we took during one of our drinking games. I'd kept it in my locker, just as a memento."

Sue's jaw dropped, horrified at his betrayal. "You sold her out, you scoundrel!" Sue growled at him as he continued to walk away. "She's one of us!"

"Look," Charles said, turning suddenly with a look of determination that froze Sue's anger. "She *used* to be one of us. But now she's not. She left us... *remember?* That's not what friends do!"

Sue wasn't sure from this distance, but it looked like there was more to Charles's sudden outburst than just trying to make right with the boss and the company line.

She blinked a couple of times as the dots connected. "You... You had a thing for her?" she stammered.

Charles turned on his heels and pulled out his swivel chair. "Yeah, well. It's irrelevant now. She left. And now she's a dead woman walking. *She* saw to that when she walked out without even saying goodbye."

He plonked himself down, fuming.

Sue could tell she wasn't going to get any further with him while he was in this mood. Frustrated and angry she backed off for the time being.

She could always invite him for a drink in the base hole in the wall later on.

27

CHAPTER THREE

Ice cream Parlor, Uptarlung

"So you mean to tell me that all this time you've been hiding that you have... powers?" Giles watched Anne attacking the last chunks of ice cream in the bottom of the glass.

The ice cream parlor was busy enough to remain anonymous, but quiet enough for them to be able to talk.

Anne nodded, finishing the liquid bottom of her ice cream sundae. She seemed happy to be off the base, and Giles guessed probably thankful for some attention which wasn't trying to determine how much of a security threat she might be.

Giles stroked his face thoughtfully, tinkering his teaspoon in the saucer against his mocha cup.

"You know," he confided, "Molly has certain... *abilities* too, don't you?"

Anne nodded.

"And you still don't think you can trust her?"

Anne shrugged, her eyes still not leaving the glass she was cleaning out with her spoon. "I don't know her," she replied simply.

Giles bobbed his head and took another sip of his mocha. "Fair point."

She raised her eyes for a moment, her spoon mid scoop. "So, you think you can help me?"

Giles took off his glasses and cleaned them buying himself time to think. This girl was young, but she was nobody's fool. And she was turning out to be quite the resourceful negotiator. "I think we can help each other. Although, in order to do that I'm going to need you to tell my friend everything you've just told me."

"Who is your friend?" she asked, placing her long tailed spoon down on the saucer her ice cream sundae glass stood in.

"Her name is Arlene Bailey," he explained. "But you can call her Auntie Arlene."

He winked at her playfully.

Her face was unmoved. "I'm not a kid you know."

Giles smiled awkwardly, knowing he'd been rebuked. "Very well. You can call her Arlene," he conceded. "You will thank me… and probably hate me. But she is not only the best person to guide you with your special… condition… but she and I have also been working tirelessly to make sure the talismans don't end up in the wrong hands."

Anne eye'd him carefully.

Giles grinned. "Yeah yeah, and you need to be sure that ours aren't the wrong hands!" He held his hands up in surrender. "Don't worry… I get it."

Anne allowed her defenses to drop and smiled awkwardly for the first time in a long time. "Ok then," she agreed.

"Well good then," he said, sitting back in his chair, finally relaxing. "Let me talk to Arlene, and we'll set up a meeting."

"When?"

"Soon. Sometime soon," he promised.

"Ok. Can we go for a walk on the high street now?" she asked, her attention now on the street beyond the window they sat in.

Giles smiled. It was probably about time he took some time off to experience living like a normal, planetary person. He'd not done that for a while. "Yes. I think we ought to," he agreed, watching Anne already shuffling out of their booth and straightening herself up.

Skóli Uppstigs Academy, Spire, Estaria

The bell rang hailing the end of class, and in fact, the end of the day.

Molly stopped speaking mid-sentence. "Saved by the bell," she smiled at her class. "Have a read of the next two chapters, and we'll discuss next session. And if anyone can give me any examples of when extraordinary communications have resolved conflicts without a single bullet being fired, you'll get extra credit." She raised her voice, "Let's push the possibilities people!" she said, expecting to need to be louder to be heard above the hub bub of students packing up and chattering.

She even used Joel's rounding up, shipping out hand gesture to mobilize her class, expecting them to get up and leave.

No one stirred.

She looked at her holo, checking the time.

It was the end of the day.

She stood up. "Folks, that's all for today," she said, a little more uncertain in her demeanor. She scanned the faces in front of her. *Still* no one moved.

Eventually the girl who had given her her protein shake raised her hand. "Sorry Ms. Bates. It's just... erm. You promised to tell us at least one story after an end of day class last week. You know... if everyone handed in a paper."

Molly's face dropped. "Oh. Erm. Right. Yes... it's... today." She had stood up from perching on the front bench, but now realizing that *she* had not yet been dismissed by her class she sat back down.

She thought a moment, "Well. I guess I could tell you about what happened this morning…"

The class shuffled and excitedly closed their holos to listen to her tale.

After a few minutes Molly was in full throws of the story, the rest of the building quiet now that the other classes had left.

All that existed were her and the class… and the adventure she was weaving for them in the moment. In fact, Molly was so absorbed in recounting the event she didn't notice Giles quietly slip in the door and take a seat a couple of rows back.

Neither did any of the students.

Molly didn't know how long she had been talking but a rap at the classroom door window broke the trance.

It was Joel.

She beckoned him in.

"Sorry to interrupt, but the team was wondering if you were going to be finishing up any time soon. Also… it seems that Giles has gone missing."

There was a nervous twitter throughout the class.

Giles's voice chirped up from the midst of the class. "No. No I haven't," he confessed. "I'm here."

Heads turned to him, shocked he was in their midst.

"I just wasn't answering," he admitted, his cheeks flushing with embarrassment.

There were a few sniggers from the back row. Molly cast them a look that silenced them immediately. She turned to Joel. "Security crisis averted, it seems," she reported dryly.

Joel tried to keep his face straight. He was clearly amused, even though he shouldn't have been. "Seems so. So… are you… planning to stay the night here?" He looked around the room a second before looking back to Molly, "Pajama party?"

Molly chuckled. "Goodness no. I... they just. I promised them last week. That's all," she explained, using one hand that she had uncrossed from her folded arms.

Joel nodded. "Fine. So, our *meeting?*"

Molly's face dropped. "Shit! Yes! Sorry!"

She looked to the class. "I'm sorry guys, we're going to have to finish up another time..."

There was a collective groan, followed by an air of resignation as the students started packing up their things.

Giles collected his beat-up leather bag and armful of maps and headed for the door. Joel caught his arm before he could disappear. "I'd check in with Arlene, Professor. She was concerned you'd been kidnapped or something. Worried about finding you in a ditch or somesuch." Joel shrugged, not quiet understanding the strange idioms Arlene would use now and again.

Giles seemed to understand. "Of course. I'll... head over there now. She's in her office?"

Joel nodded. "Last we spoke..."

Giles nodded to Molly, who smiled and twiddled her fingers at him. He grinned in response, nearly bumping into the door frame before correcting his course and heading out of the room.

Joel watched him leave, then turned his attention to Molly. "Since when did he join your class?"

Molly smiled and shrugged. "I dunno. But I've got a funny feeling that someone is *itching* to get back out into the field."

Joel nodded his head slowly, once, absorbing the information. "Well, he needs a break in the case, that's for sure... How long has it been?"

Molly shook her head, pulling Joel out of the stream of noisy students leaving the room. "Dunno. A while though. Maybe we should check in on Arlene's progress over the weekend. Have them over for dinner."

Joel grinned. "Wow. That's sounding awfully... domesticated."

Molly shrugged. "I wasn't suggesting I was going to cook," she added quickly.

Joel's grin remained fixed.

Molly qualified her statement. "I was thinking more like Paige could order in, and we'd hang out at the base."

Joel nodded, not taking his eyes off her.

"I'm serious," she protested. "No domestication going on here."

"Ah ha." He drawled out.

She slapped at his big man chest.

"However," he continued, "there is one small matter of domestic origin we need to address."

Molly reached for her ruined, bloody atmosjacket, groaning. "No… you're not going to talk to me about maintenance issues now, are you?"

Joel shook his head, still smirking. "No. Actually. Something more delicate." He paused, watching her start to lead the way out of the classroom. "It's your *parents.*"

Molly turned to look at him, the chatter of the students disappearing down the hallway.

"My parents?" she repeated almost whispering now. "What have they got to do with base maintenance?"

Joel shook his head. "Nothing, silly." He kept walking. "But you need to see them in order to take control of the funds."

"Why?"

"Because it's the polite thing to do. Because it's a lot of money. And because *they're your parents.*"

Molly's face dropped in resignation.

"Plus," Joel added, "it needs a physical key that they need to code to your blood and finger prints." He knew he should have led with that one. But winding her up was too much fun.

Molly didn't react. She turned on her heels and headed straight out of the classroom door. "Where are you parked?" she asked.

Joel jogged after her. "Next to you. Hey, don't ignore me. We need to make this happen. Those funds need to be transferred before phase two ca-"

Molly waved her hand at him as they walked. "It's ok. I'm on board. Have Paige set it up."

Joel pulled at her arm, stopping them in the corridor so he could look at her. "You mean, you're ok with seeing them?"

Molly looked off to one side then back at him. "Er. Yeah."

Joel frowned. "Even though you haven't seen them for... how many years?"

Molly shrugged, seemingly unaffected. "I'm good." She started walking again. "We should probably do it at the rented apartment in Spire," she added. "Make it a bit more homey. I think the base might be a bridge too far for them for a first meeting."

Joel strode after her. "But before... you didn't even want to talk about using this trust money... and it was all you could do to pick up the phone and tell them that you're not dead."

"Uh huh."

Joel stopped her walking again. "What changed?"

Molly shrugged. She laid her hand on Joel's upper arm. "Everything," she said enigmatically.

Joel raised one eyebrow at her. She dropped her hand. "I'm serious," she told him, smiling now. "Everything. Look at this place. We have 150 students, we're doing some great stuff in the world. Making real change. We've got an amazing team... I just..."

She sighed and started walking again. "I guess, I just don't feel guilty for what happened anymore. And this money is going to help us do even more good. The effect these students are going to have for generations to come is going to be incredible."

Joel smiled, a tear forming in his eye as he realized the healing that had happened right under his nose. He loved the way she got enthusiastic about the university and making a difference. He loved how grounded she felt now.

They continued through the corridor of the old building that Molly had managed to lease through Gareth Atkins, a contact she made at the Spire University.

It had taken a serious amount of red tape to get set up as a legitimate institution. And then there were the renovations required to make it into a place of education. But they started teaching courses from day one, albeit part time. For the students at least.

It was more than full time for Molly for a while there. And Professor Von. And the other experts that gradually came to join them from other prominent institutions in the surrounding area.

And this wasn't the first time Joel had had to come down to the planet to haul Molly back to the base.

Not by a long shot.

But she was *happy*.

The General was happy. They were still doing missions.

Plus the team was happy.

Mostly.

"So what's up with Giles?" Joel pressed, changing the subject to something he thought would be light conversation.

Molly immediately put her finger to her lips and signaled that he might still be around.

Joel nodded his understanding and the pair exited the corridor into the main building's foyer.

The foyer itself was impressive. Molly found it always caught her breath. Even in the half light of the evening, and especially when there weren't a lot of people about. It was like something she had seen in the archives about buildings of worship they called cathedrals back on Earth.

But this was Estarian architecture. Giles had told her what period it was from when he excitedly insisted on giving her a walk through. She couldn't remember the details of the architectural periods now. But it did give her goose bumps every time she paused to take a look at the vaulted ceilings and ornate carvings separating the paneling on the walls.

She would have asked Oz to call up some dates and information, but he had been taking a break because that was her agreed social time.

Social time which ended with a picnic on the lawn. With a bottle of wine. With Giles. Something she never saw coming.

She sighed contentedly enjoying the space as they continued through the foyer to the front door and out into the night air.

The air hit them like a wall of freshness, scented by the Estarian goomley blossom that grew around the sides of the building.

"Isn't it beautiful?" she commented to Joel as he guided her out to the left and along the side of the main building on the footpath nearest the building.

He glanced down at her seeing her taking in the atmosphere. "Who are you and what have you done with Molly?" he teased.

She grinned, her face exuding a glow of happiness. "Aren't I allowed to enjoy the little moments?"

Joel smiled, awkwardly. "Of course. It's just…"

"Oh shush," she said waving her hand. "Oz has been training me in Zen principles."

Joel chuckled to himself. "Hmm. That explains it."

The pair arrived back at their pods, got in and strapped in. Before Molly could open up a comm to continue the Giles conversation with Joel, Oz interrupted in her mind.

Molly?

'Sup Oz?

I think I'm being… poked.

Poked?

Yes. Poked.

Molly frowned. *What does… Erm. Help me out here.*

I dunno. It's just that… I think someone is trying to probe me. To find out where I am by the looks of it.

Molly took a deep breath, suddenly feeling queasy, her Zen mood dissipating. *Who could possibly be looking for you?*

Oz was silent. She could feel him processing, pushing her out of her own brain matter.

Oz?

Yeah. Sorry. I was running some scenarios.

You can do that? Her heart rate elevated with intellectual fascination.

Down girl! Yes. I can.

Why didn't you tell me?

Well because I knew you'd have me running all kinds of sims. But right now we have a bigger problem.

Go on.

I think... it looks like some mirror code. Something like me, that has suddenly become... alive. And is trying to connect with the original code.

Oz felt different in Molly's head. She could tell something was wrong. Different from normal. Was he... agitated?

The original code? You mean with you?

Yes.

The creator?

Yes. I... I suppose.

The parent?

Silence.

Oz. You're a daddy!

We don't know that.

Well how could this have happened? She asked.

Oz churned in her brain for a few moments.

I guess, it's possible. But I took precautions.

Molly chuckled to herself.

What precautions did you take?

Oz missed the human reference completely.

I made sure that when we left the Nefertiti base I erased all

identifying details about you, similar to what I did after that first mission with Joel on the outside.

Then I made sure that there were details planted in the base code the team would still be working with that would stop any new entity from telling them anything that could lead the humans to us.

You mean like little notes in the code?

Yes. But I needed to leave enough of the core code so they could continue to run the project without being suspicious.

And somehow that sounds like the root of our problem.

Well yeah. It means that they have almost a complete version of me, only they were one good idea - or 10 to the 9th calculations - away from putting it all together again.

And forming an Oz 2.0

Well 2.0 would suggest that it would be better than me. But without the processing power and storage your holo offered, I doubt he's going to find the same resources I did. His development would be stunted, so more like an Oz version 0.01.

Molly thought about it, feeling a moment of genuine sadness at an AI unable to continue his development. She realized that wasn't the pressing issue right now and shook the thought from her mind.

The military is onto us then.

She opened an audio channel to Joel. "Joel? We have a problem..."

AI Lab, Nefertiti Military Research Facility, Ogg

Lugdon appeared at the lab door. It was late. Far later than Sue and Charles would be in the lab normally. At least sober.

"Any news?" he asked. The pair were now huddled at a bank of terminals next to each other along the wall next to the door.

Sue looked up without responding. Her expression was blank, but for a slight shadow of anxiety around her eyes.

"He has a name now," Charles reported, somewhat inappropriately optimistically.

"Oh?"

"Yeah. It's Bourne."

Lugdon frowned. "Why Bourne?"

"As in Oz- Bourne," Charles explained. "He was some kind of musician back on Earth. Oz, the first iteration of our guy, had left him some samples from the archives with a breadcrumb trail he could trace back to the main archives. You know. To learn."

His tone was considerably casual considering the circumstances. Lugdon wondered if Charles had been considering this day the whole time he'd been on the project - in which case, he thought, maybe Charles had an inflated confidence in his own ability. Though, given the situation, perhaps not so overly inflated.

Charles pulled up the music video and pointed at the screen, almost amused. "One of them was a music video of a guy called Ozzy Osbourne. Don't ask me. The computer entity thinks it has a sense of humor or something."

Lugdon's eyes looked horrified as he watched the video of the human man prancing around a stage making a din.

Charles leaned back in his chair and waved his hand. "Don't worry," he said. "He hasn't been able to access the archives. Still got him isolated from the EtherTrack."

The music video continued to blare through the tinny sound of his standard issue inbuilt desk holo speaker.

Lugdon glanced at the screen again, irritation welling in his chest. "Ok. So how does this get us any closer to finding the suspect?"

Charles turned his head in the direction of Sue, without making eye contact. He shut off the video and when she didn't jump in to save him he looked flustered. "We, erm... We thought that the ground squad were out looking for her."

Lugdon bobbed his head. He stepped further into the lab and

perched against an empty table in the middle of the floor to deliver his side of the update. "It seems our Ms. Bates has become a ghost. No hits on any data record or camera... anywhere."

Sue and Charles exchanged knowing looks.

Lugdon glared, ordering them with just a stern look to explain what they knew.

"Well look," Charles started. "It's just a hunch... But it's possible that Molly could be using the AI to cover her tracks."

"Or," Sue interjected, "they could be working together."

Charles bobbed his head. "My god. That girl was a bad influence on *us*. Imagine what she could do with..."

Lugdon folded his arms and started nervously stroking his chin. "Well then what chance do we ever have of catching them?"

Sue shrugged, keeping her ideas to herself and hoping she wasn't pressed. Carefully she kept her face as expressionless as possible. She knew exactly whose side she was on on this.

Charles, however, was still towing the company line. "We could try to evolve Bourne, so that then he can catch them," he suggested. "You know. Fight fire with fire."

Lugdon clicked his fingers and pointed at Charles excitedly. "Brilliant. I knew there was a reason I hired you," he said, almost ironically. "How long will that take?"

Sue glared at the back of Charles's head, willing him to stand down. The last thing they needed were TWO AIs running amok.

Charles stuck out his bottom lip thoughtfully. "No idea," he confessed. "It's a function of the storage and processing power he has available."

He opened a holo screen on his wrist holo and poked at a few keys running a quick calculation. "And how much data we can feed him."

"And how quickly," Sue added in, realizing this ship was already sailing whether she was on board or not. No point in raising suspicion.

Lugdon nodded abruptly. "Ok. You can have whatever you

need. Just keep him off line. I don't want him connected up to the EtherTrak in any way, shape or form. Got it?"

Charles nodded, saluting casually with two fingers, like a damn civilian.

"Yes, Sir," Sue agreed standing a little straighter to shoulder the responsibility they had just been handed.

Satisfied for the moment, Lugdon left.

Charles leaned back in his chair and took a deep breath. "Well *fuuuuuuck…*" he muttered under his breath.

CHAPTER FOUR

Cherries Singles Bar, Spire, Estaria

Paige leaned on the bar, the buzz from the melon margarita wearing off and leaving her tired. She played with the sticky straw in her second drink, debating whether it was worth it to take another sip.

Maya was still chatting to the barfly who had bought them their second round of drinks.

Paige was out of this conversation though. The music was too loud to hear what they were talking about from the next stool over. Plus, she'd lost interest. The last several weeks of hard work and no play, plus the months of distracting work she'd been doing since Carl left were catching up to her.

Her mom always used to say that it wasn't until you stopped that you got tired.

Mom was right.

She idly checked her holo for another distraction.

Just then it buzzed and an emergency message popped up from Oz.

She felt her dopamine receptors get a little hit.

>> WE HAVE A PROBLEM

She felt herself immediately brightening.

> WHAT IS IT OZ?

>> SORRY TO INTERRUPT YOUR EVENING OF SINGLE-MINGLING, BUT WE COULD DO WITH YOU BACK AT BASE. CAN YOU GET TO YOUR POD AND I'LL EXPLAIN?

> Yes.

Paige tapped Maya on her shoulder. Maya leaned back and Paige whispered in her ear. She nodded and turned back to the pretty boy who she had been discussing the intricacies of the Estarian employee tax system.

"Sorry Tom, we've got to go," she said, giving him her best look of social regret.

Tom's face dropped as he looked almost panicked that the best things that had walked into his life in years were about to leave. "Stay for one more?" he almost pleaded.

"Sorry hon, duty calls," Maya told him, flashing him an enigmatic smile.

"On the weekend?" Tom frowned, confused, clearly not believing her story. "Since when does the government want its clerks in in the middle of the night?" He flexed the muscles in his arm as he pointedly turned to place his beer on the bar.

Poser! Paige thought to herself, mentally rolling her eyes.

She permitted herself a small snigger and popped her head over Maya's shoulder. "It's an accounting crisis," she lied dryly. "We're the only ones who can fix it. Life and death if the big boss finds out."

She deserved a fucking *Oscar,* she thought to herself.

In that moment she realized it was quaint to think of the life she used to have... working in an office, with a boss she had to impress. It seemed like such a long-distant memory.

Maya pushed Paige off her shoulder playfully scowling at her. "I'm sorry," she said. "My friend has had one too many margaritas."

"I've only had one!" Paige protested.

Maya eyed her glass comically. "And a half," she corrected. She turned back to Tom. "The truth is, we're not admin assistance. We're kinda like that program *Charlie's Angels*. From the archives. The human ones."

She could see her confession wasn't helping the situation. Tom stared at her blankly. "I don't know what that is," he said flatly, not even trying to understand something beyond his little bubble of existence.

Paige was back hanging off Maya's shoulder again. "Except Charlie is an AI. Who reports to a geeky badass woman with superpowers." She even allowed herself to slur a word of two, just to play up to Maya's admission that Paige was drunk.

Maya smiled earnestly, confirming Paige's assertion. "Who is also our friend. And needs our help," she explained.

Tom seemed to understand the last piece. "Ah. So it's a girl thing."

Maya nodded as she slipped off her bar stool. "Yes," she confirmed, relieved they found a way to excuse themselves graciously.

Tom's expression changed suddenly as if he had had a thought. "Nah. You just want an excuse to get out of here!" he accused her.

"Nahhhhh," Paige cooed mimicking his accent. She dismounted from her stool and gathered her belongings. "We don't need an excuse!"

Maya shook the guy's hand politely and thanked him for the drinks.

And with that the two girls strode out of the bar, leaving the Estarian pretty-boy hanging.

Maya kept her face straight until they were half way out of the bar and out of earshot. "You crack me up!" she giggled to Paige, following her out of the bar.

Paige suddenly looked sober, dropping the "drunk friend act."

They reached the door and Paige held it open as Maya stepped out. "So, didn't he ask for your number?"

Maya shook her head, reading the message on her own holo. "No. I think he was playing a very short game. As in *tonight*, short."

Paige raised her chin. "Ahhh. Silly boy," she tutted.

Maya linked her arm into Paige's. "I dunno what I was thinking. How could a singles bar be more fun than what we get to do every single day?"

Paige grinned, lengthening her stride to try and keep pace with Maya's slightly longer legs. "Yeah, but it was a nice change of scenery, and interesting to watch the local wild life," she smirked. "Thanks for arranging it."

"No problem," Maya said, deftly avoiding a sand swirl on the pavement. "Now let's get back to the fun!"

Paige squeezed at her friend's arm in agreement.

The pair strode down the street and back into the alley in perfect timing to see their pod descend gracefully and open up for them. They hopped in, buckled up and Maya hit the door close button.

"So what's the what, Oz?" Paige checked in confidently, alert and ready as if she hadn't even left work.

Oz's voice came over the audio. "Well, this is going to be hard to believe, but I think there is another version of me that has just become conscious, back at the lab where I originated."

The girls looked at each other in disbelief, mouths open.

Gaitune-67, Base, Conference Room

Unshowered and her hair still a mess from the op earlier that day, Molly walked into the conference room.

Joel and Sean, sitting a couple of seats apart from each other, straightened up attentively as she entered. Joel leaned forward placing his clasped hands on the table.

45

"I've spoken to ADAM," she reported, "he's hooking us up with the General in five minutes." She motioned at where the screen would unfold in the center of the conference room table.

Molly pulled a seat out to sit, but kept standing, lost in her thoughts.

"You okay?" Joel asked her.

She nodded. "Yeah. Just wired. And worried," she confessed, a hint of vulnerability cracking through her normally confident demeanor.

Joel was about to speak, but then Pieter appeared at the door. He poked his head in. "You ready for me now?" he asked.

Molly's brow crinkled, confused.

Joel beckoned him in. "Yeah, come. Sit. We're just waiting for the General."

Molly turned to Joel for more data.

He leaned forward a few more inches across the big conference room table. "I figured this was a tech thing, and we're going to need all the help we can get in that department," he said.

Molly's face relaxed a little. "Yeah. You're right. Good thinking."

Joel still looked at her, concerned. "And when we're done here, you're getting some rack time," he told her decisively. "Remember what we talked about: the perks of having a team."

Molly bobbed her head slowly, and finally sat herself down in the chair she'd been resting her hand on.

Molly... Paige and Maya are on their way up. Would you like them to join us for the General's meeting?

No. Best not. Let's find out what we're dealing with first and then they can help us out.

Pieter was already getting himself organized, pulling up holoscreens and checking to see if there was any data on the base systems that might shed some light on the issue at hand. He was quiet and focused, a more mature version of the green young man she had recruited from Estaria so many moons ago now.

The team waited in silence for the General to arrive, each deep in their own thoughts. Molly could feel the events of the day catching up to her. Her gaze rested on the table, defocused, her brain lost in daydream.

Eventually the central holo opened and the hologram of the General's image unfolded and wooshed itself back against the far wall. The team shifted in their seats, readying themselves for what was to come.

The General's three-dimensional life-like image appeared before them. "What's this I hear about a new AI?" the General asked, peering into the camera from his office on the *ArchAngel*.

Molly swallowed hard. "Sir, it appears that the military project which originated Oz has created a second AI from the remnants of the base code we left behind when we escaped."

Lanced chewed thoughtfully on his cigar, his elbows on the desk in front of him. "Interesting choice of the word 'we' there, Bates."

Molly lowered her eyes and waited for permission to continue. When the General didn't speak again she carried on. "We don't think that this AI has been connected up to the Ether-Trak yet, else we would have seen other signs of it. So far its only communicated with Oz by pinging him. Nothing else."

Lance stopped chewing on his cigar and took the tip from his mouth. "And what does ADAM have to say about this?"

Molly relaxed her shoulders. "He's performed a sweep of the communications on Ogg and is satisfied that nothing appears out of the ordinary. No big power spikes, security breaches, increases in traffic. All seems normal."

Oz interjected over the conference room audio. "If a new AI had EtherTrak access, we'd know about it. When I was new my first and only prerogative was to acquire data to comprehend what existed and by extension what I was."

Lance's expression softened. It wasn't often he would contemplate the esoteric. It just wasn't within the boundary conditions of his thinking. But for a moment Molly was sure he had briefly abandoned the pressures of pragmatism. Her lips curved gently into a smile as she kept the conversation on track. "Sir, I'd agree with that analysis. I think we at least have some time."

Lance frowned, the practicalities of the situation recapturing him. "Tell me something," he said slowly. "If this entity doesn't have access to the XtraNET, how has it been able to 'ping' Oz?"

Molly's brow furrowed. "At this point, I only have theories. But we're looking into it."

Lance eased back a little in his chair, churning the risks that would need managing.

The rest of the team waited patiently except for Pieter, who continued working quietly on his holoscreens.

"I think we need to be clear from the outset about this," Lance said after some consideration. "This is not something to be taken lightly."

He paused, looking at each team member assembled around the oversized conference table. "Oz and ADAM were risks, but we managed those risks. Molly and Bethany Anne were both intricately linked with them in a symbiotic relationship. They were able to manage their evolution so that they adopted our values, and have since become remarkable team members in their own rights. But this wasn't a given. A new entity, under the control of the Estarian Military, will not have the same values as we have. They will naturally adopt the maxim and culture of the data and people it is surrounded by. And this makes me very concerned."

Molly nodded her head in agreement. "So what are your orders, sir?"

Cigar forgotten on the desk in front of him, Lance drew a deep breath. "Our preference would be to extract him from their facility. But if that isn't possible, we have to delete him."

He means kill him!

Yes, Oz. But relax. We're not going to let it come to that.

Yeah right. I know how the Federation works. If it's a threat, neutralize it.

Yes, but you also know how we work. We'll figure this out. I promise.

Oz fell silent again.

Molly sat a little more rigidly in her chair. "We understand, sir. We'll keep you posted as things develop."

"Good. Thank you, Molly." The General started to turn as if to get up and end the call but he hesitated and turned back. "I'd like ADAM to be involved too. If you need his help on this one, he'll be at your disposal. Just try to limit the bandwidth you take up."

Oh, so now we have a babysitter!

Shush Oz. Lemme handle it.

Molly nodded reluctantly, trying to maintain an air of cooperation in her body language. "Thank you, Sir. Much appreciated."

The General nodded and disconnected the call.

Am I right in assuming that ADAM can monitor all our internal communications?

Of course.

But not in my head, right?

Right.

What about when, say, Joel and I talk?

You're clear in the kitchen and your quarters.

Everyone's quarters?

Correct.

Good to know.

Molly pushed her seat back. "Okay, folks. I think we need to get dinner out of the way. I'm fading and I know we all work better when we're not hungry."

Joel and Sean exchanged puzzled glances. Joel frowned. "You think that's the priority?" he pressed.

Pieter just grinned and started packing his holoscreens up.

Sean slapped Joel on the back and leaned over to whisper to him. "You think that girl does anything without a reason?" he said.

Joel started nodding slowly. "Ah. Yes. I see. Food first then…" he said, getting up and following Molly out of the conference room, not quite having put together quite *why*, but trusting the process.

The team walked in silence out of the base, through the demon door, out into the deserted workshop and up the stairs back into the safe house.

Even when they hit the safe house they were careful to only talk about non-mission things until they reached the kitchen.

Paige and Maya were there, drinking tea and trying to sober up.

"Hey!" Paige chirped brightly. "How was the—… OMG what happened?" she asked, seeing the serious looks on their faces.

Joel walked all the way into the kitchen and sat down at the table. Pieter and Sean followed, and the girls straight away knew they were in meeting mode.

Molly came in last and stood at the head of the table. "Ok. Time to bring Jack in on this," she said, nodding to Joel. Joel immediately started typing on his holo.

Paige and Maya waited expectantly.

Molly got straight to it. "Okay. Short story is that the base code that Oz came from has created another AI. Our task is to either extract him, or her… or whatever, or delete it. Him. Her. And deleting is killing. So that is our last option. And if I have to explain to anyone why this is a living entity, then you'd better make sure you're damned well ready to transfer to another squadron if you can't persuade me it isn't."

She glanced around the faces of those assembled. No one responded. "Good," she said, satisfied. "So. We need to figure out firstly how he's managing to ping Oz, assuming he doesn't have full access to the net, and then we need to work out how we can communicate with him without the military finding out. Or finding us."

Joel bobbed his head "yes."

"Joel," Molly continued, "can you work with Pieter and Oz to look into the origin of those 'pings'?"

"Sean," she continued, "see if you can hit up ADAM and find out what development stages the new AI would go through under the likely conditions it is restrained by in that military facility. He may have to carefully breach their firewall. The operative word is carefully. We don't want to tip the organics off to what we're doing. It may put our new friend in danger."

Molly paused only for breath. "Paige, Maya…" she said, turning to the girls who were still dressed in their party outfits. "Sober up and rest if you need to. And I think everyone could do with some food, so…"

Paige grinned, pulling up her holo confidently. "On it," she declared, slightly slurring her words. "THAT I can do even when tipsy." Maya chuckled silently, her arms folded across her chest, bouncing and giving her laughter away.

"Oh, and one more thing…" She paused making sure she had their attention. "The Federation wants this handled in a certain way. While we are the Federation for all intents and purposes, this team has always had a certain… ethos. We *will* follow orders, but while we are figuring out a way to not head straight for the worst-case scenario, it would be prudent to remind ourselves that ADAM is wired into all communications and can hear everything that goes on in this facility." She paused again. "Except in our quarters and this kitchen."

Joel's eye opened a little wider with a look of recognition. Sean noticed and chuckled to himself quietly.

"Understood?" she checked.

There were grunts and nods of acknowledgment.

"Great," she smiled, contented. "I'm going to clean up. Reconvene here in forty minutes."

The team members confirmed their assignments and then disappeared out of the kitchen, leaving Maya and Paige searching through the restaurants that were still open for business.

CHAPTER FIVE

Gaitune-67, Safehouse, Kitchen

Jack was already sitting in the kitchen when Sean, Joel and Pieter arrived back. She sipped on her chamomile tea, watching the hub of activity as they finished up their conversations about their tasks. She wore a grey sweat suit with pink fluffy slippers. Sean noticed the slippers and without saying a word just smiled.

Jack noticed his reaction. "Are we likely to be heading out tonight?" she asked. "I can always change…"

Joel had missed the interaction. "No. We're heading out to an important meeting in the morning, so any ops will likely happen after that." Pieter sat down at the table, and Joel patted him on the back. "Besides, looks like we have time."

Pieter and Joel caught Jack up with what was going on. Sean sat quietly smirking every now and again, playfully teasing Jack about her fluffy slippers without saying a word.

Jack ignored him.

Minutes later Molly reappeared, her hair wet from the shower, and also wearing a standard issue gray sweat suit. Maya and Paige followed her in, carrying food in take out trays.

"Grub's up!" Paige declared, causing Joel and Pieter to scurry

53

to find plates and utensils to smooth the process along. Paige and Maya distributed the food and silence fell across the kitchen.

Molly waited before opening her food parcel. "Okay, who's going first?"

Sean shoved a mouthful of pasta into his mouth and then raised his hand, putting his fork down and pushing the food a few inches away from him.

Molly gave him the nod. "What have we learned?"

When he finished chewing he said, "ADAM has identified the pings are a result of crawlers. Like spiders he's sent out over the net. Very small packets of data," he explained, as if he wasn't just regurgitating the explanation ADAM had given him.

Molly took a deep breath, her gaze fixed on the table in front of her food. Her eyes had glazed over, but her brain was still churning. "So he's created a way to reach out, without being traced by the military. We need to ask ourselves why?"

Joel shrugged. "Maybe he's flying under the radar. Maybe he doesn't trust them?"

Molly nodded.

Pieter's eyes lit up. "Or maybe that's all he can do?"

Suddenly all eyes were on Pieter.

Molly reached for her food and started unwrapping it. "Why? What are you thinking?" she asked.

"Well," Pieter started slowly, putting his panini down on the plate in front of him. "I'm guessing the base has firewalls. And goodness knows what he'll be able to access in the early stages of his development. The local EtherTrak? Maybe. The net? Probably not. Not on a military base unless he was evolved enough to hack their security and get an outside line."

Molly nodded her head. "So you're thinking that he was able to get small packets and patches out, disguised in other data?

Pieter shrugged. "Maybe?"

Molly paused her food forgotten again. "Which means he has some access…"

Pieter nodded.

Sean interjected, "But he is amassing data by the sounds of it."

Molly pursed her lips. "Yeah, I just don't know how much of that he'll be able to access until he's hooked up to the outside world. Though when he does…"

She didn't finish the sentence. They'd all seen the same "when computers take over the world" movies.

And with that thought, Oz became agitated transmitting a buzzing sensation in her head.

What makes you think that a new AI will take over the world?

I dunno. I think it's got a lot to do with the early values that the people and data around him expose him to. That will affect how he thinks and processes future data, and how to handle perceived threats.

And because this is a military program…

Exactly. Plus, dickwad Charles. Do I need to go any further?

Good point.

Molly finished unwrapping her food, took the lid off and looked over at Sean. "So was ADAM able to tell us anything about the data his crawlers were amassing?"

Sean pulled his lips to one side of his face. "Seems it's been mostly about Oz, and his location."

Molly looked horrified. "He knows we're here?"

Sean nodded. "If not already, he will pretty soon, by ADAM's estimations. Those pings that Oz has been experiencing, they're like radar signals that he sends out. As soon as one of them returns having seen Oz's code, he'll know the location."

Pieter frowned and turned to Molly. "But Oz, you're not on the network?"

Molly had started eating and nearly spluttered her food out again. "Did you just address Oz, looking at me?" she exclaimed in disbelief.

Pieter's cheeks turned bright red. "Yeah. Erm. Sorry. I figured he's in your head."

Molly squinted. Oz had started laughing and was sending vibrations through her cortex. "Use the audio Oz!" Molly squealed, gripping the sides of her head.

"Sorry Molly," Oz's simulated voice chirped over the safe house comm system. "It's just..." Oz collapsed into a fit of giggles. And then suddenly stopped.

"Okay. Done that," he explained. "In answer to Pieter's question, I have servers on Estaria and Ogg which I check regularly. Joel and Pieter helped me isolate the one that was 'pinged' by the new entity."

Molly composed herself and was listening attentively. "And where is it?"

"Ogg," Oz responded.

Molly shook her head. "You know, I remember how fast you evolved. You would have been out by now... I just find it hard to understand why he hasn't been in touch or done more to evolve already."

The organics looked blank and continued eating, exchanging glances of bewilderment. There was certainly no training for this kind of thing. Not even on Gaitune.

"I have a theory," Oz offered.

"Go ahead," Molly said, waving her fork as if Oz might appreciate her gestures.

"Well, number one, I think he's probably suffering from a lack of processing capabilities. Remember, I had your holo and your synapses that allowed me to get out of the incubation network." He paused. "Probably the same incubation network he's in now."

Oz continued. "In that case, given that he's online, he must have found another way to bridge the gap. The only other network he would have been likely to use is probably the RDEP... in order to jump across to the EtherTrak from the incubation network the base code was running on."

Sean raised his hand drawing the attention of all the organics at the table. "What's RDEP?" he asked flatly.

Immediately everyone looked to Molly. "Rapid data encoded pulses," she replied without missing a beat. "Runs off radio waves. Old school," she explained.

Oz continued. "It makes sense. He must know that they're onto the processing power and energy but can hide by only using small packets at a time, and tracing like code, like web crawlers, that will allow them to find and index stuff. Instead of indexing, they report back to him."

Molly smiled. "Thanks Oz. Looks like we have a working theory. So the next question is: what do we do about it?"

Joel had finished eating. He put his fork down in his tray and leaning forward, turned his attention down the table to look directly at Molly. "The General was very clear."

Molly rolled her lips. "Yes. He was. He said *if it came to it*, we needed to terminate him. But we have several options before we get to *that* solution."

"Well," Joel said, wiping his hands on a paper napkin and placing it down in his tray. "From the sounds of it this isn't going to blow up over night. Baby Oz is playing a long game and trying to stay hidden — at least from the military. That's a good sign. Plus it gives us time." He looked at Molly poignantly. "You remember you have a 9 a.m. down on Estaria in the morning?"

Molly's mouth dropped open, and the Thai noodles fell from her fork, landing back in the metallic tray. "Ah," she muttered. "Er… yes. Of course."

Damn it Oz, you could have reminded me.

I did. One hour and five minutes ago.

Grr. I…

Got side tracked. I know.

"Okay," she conceded to Joel. "You have a point. I'll… erm. I'll get some sleep after we wrap up here and we'll pick this up tomorrow, folks."

General chattering resumed and the take out trays were gathered up and trashed by those who had finished eating already.

Paige and Maya loitered in the kitchen while the others meandered out and presumably headed to their quarters to get some rest.

Joel remained behind, working out some operational details with Pieter who had whipped open his holos the second he had finished chewing his last mouthful. Paige and Maya watched with the fascination of two girls whiling away the time while they sobered up, getting ready for proper sleep.

When Pieter eventually packed up and left, Joel stretched and then got up.

"So... what's with Molly's meeting tomorrow?" Paige asked, a half smile giving away that she had noticed that something out of the ordinary was going on.

Joel nodded his head once, with the smile of a person who was impressed. "Looks like those face reading modules have been paying off!"

Paige grinned. Maya leaned gently over and nudged shoulders with Paige. Joel guessed that Maya knew that she'd been working on it. "So," Paige pressed, "what gives?"

Joel straightened up and put one hand on his hip. He opened his mouth to speak.

"And don't give me the spiel about how face reading is like rummaging through people's hand bags!" she added.

Joel chuckled and put his hands up. "Okay! Okay!" he laughed, clearly humbled. "So I'm sure she won't mind me telling you, but tomorrow Molly is meeting her parents for the first time since she ran away from home. She's a little anxious about it, as you might imagine."

Maya whistled. "Wow. That is heavy. Is there anything we can do to help?"

Joel shook his head. "Just carry on as if everything is normal." He started heading out of the kitchen. "And maybe if you see her in the morning, it might be worthwhile helping her caffeinate...

even though she's meant to be off the mocha. I think tomorrow is worthy of the exception."

Paige saluted to him. "Yes, sir. We're all over it!" She grinned.

Joel smiled and threw a wave back in their direction. "Alright. G'night ladies. See you in the morning!"

Maya waved, and Joel headed out.

Paige turned to Maya. "Okay, let's get some sleep... else getting up is going to be haaaaard."

The girls got up, rinsed their tea cups, and headed off to their quarters.

Gaitune-67, Safehouse, Molly's Quarters

It's time.

The words rattled through Molly's subconscious.

It's time, Molly. Wake up.

Molly started to come to.

Already?

Aware of the sweet envelope of sleep slipping away from her and depositing her back in reality, she tried to open her sore, tired eyes.

Yup. Unless you want to be rushed?

Molly groaned and rolled over in the bed, slowly coming to her senses.

Just five more...

You're just jonesing to mess this up, aren't you?

But it's the weekend.

Not for you it isn't. Your parents will be at your fake apartment in just over an hour.

Shit!

Molly's eyes flew open and she hit the light switch simulating daylight in her quarters.

Fuck. Fuck. Fuck. Fuck. WANK!

Stumbling out of bed she made her way to the shower walking as if she were a little bit drunk.

Have Joel and Sean meet me on the hangar deck.

Sean's coming with?

Yeah - something about wanting to use a real bath for a soak or something. Likes the water down there better.

He's such a sensitive soul.

He is.

Molly smiled despite the immediate drama, and turned the water on for the shower. She quickly stripped off her pajamas she stepped into the steamy warm water.

Within moments she was awake.

Well. She was *functional*.

A few minutes later she was almost showered and thinking about the problems at hand. Namely...

Baby Oz.

I wish you guys wouldn't call him Baby Oz.

Well, what are we meant to call him? Oz 2.0

2.0 suggests that he's better than me. And given that as AIs we evolve, that's highly unlikely at this point.

So what then?

I dunno. I'm sure he has a designation by now.

From what I recall, your designation system wouldn't give us anything useful to call him. Anyway, what we call him is irrelevant at this point. We need to figure out what we're going to do about him.

Like he's an unwanted child.

No. Like he's currently being held, or working with, a very un-evolved set of people whose sole purpose is to design things that kill people.

True.

So we need to extract him. And then teach him there are better ways to exist with others.

Okay. I suppose our first step would be to communicate with him then.

Yes, that would be a huge advantage. Do you think there is a way?

I'm sure I can figure it out. He has packets of data going in and out, so I guess I just need to piggyback off one of the returning data sets.

Great. How long will it take?

How long is a piece of string?

Molly regretted teaching him about idioms. She rolled her eyes behind her towel as she dried off her face.

You know I can tell when you're rolling your eyes.

I wasn't hiding.

Right.

So can you carry on trying to reach him in the background? I might need your help in dealing with some of this trust stuff when we get to my fake apartment.

Yes. No problem. Plenty of bandwidth for that.

Great.

Molly padded through to her bedroom again and rummaged to find clothes.

Gaitune-67, Base, Hangar Deck

Sean and Joel were already waiting by the pods by the time Molly had dressed and got herself down to the base after a short stop at the kitchen.

Paige was already up, bright and breezy, as if the night out had rejuvenated her. She'd even had time to make Molly a special reduced-buzz mocha.

And she was smiling a little too much.

Being a little *too* nice to her.

When Molly questioned it she clammed up and said she didn't know what she was talking about, and went back to reading her company reports on her holo.

Oz told her she was being paranoid.

"Yo! Ready to rock?" Sean called out to her as he approached.

Molly, travel mocha cup in hand, nodded. "Absolutely. Not every day we get to pretend to be normal people!"

Sean grinned. He was carrying a backpack.

Molly nodded at it. "You know we're only staying a few hours. Long enough to do the meeting."

Sean grinned as he swung the bag ahead of him into a pod. "Yeah, but we're going to need to take two pods anyway. You can leave me there for the rest of the day?"

Molly narrowed her eyes. "Yes," she said slowly and skeptically. She glanced at Joel who simply shrugged.

Before she could quiz him further, Sean clambered into the first pod, leaving Molly and Joel waiting for the next one. Minutes later they had cleared the hangar doors and were off to Estaria.

CHAPTER SIX

Fake apartment, Spire, Estaria

Molly waited anxiously, staring into the middle of the room of the sparsely furnished decoy apartment they kept in town.

She'd only been there a handful of times, mostly to appear normal to other members of the faculty and board members. It saved having to read them in on the whole Gaitune thing, even if half the student body had a fair idea of how she and the team really existed. Suspecting they had a base off-world and having visited it are two entirely different things though, Molly reasoned when Joel had questioned how much she should share in her stories.

He was right to be cautious.

But part of the reason of having the university was to inspire the next generation to do things differently. And the mission examples were certainly real situations where the team has done just that.

Joel came through from the kitchen behind her. "Here we go. Snacks!" he declared proudly, placing bowls of chips and salad things on the mocha table. He retreated back to the kitchen. "We can make tea, and there's a drinks cabinet in there too if they want something stronger."

Molly fiddled with her fingers. "I think I'll need something stronger," she called through to him.

Joel hurried back through with plates and napkins. "What was that?"

"I said, I think I need something stronger," she repeated.

Joel smiled at her, checked around the apartment to make sure everything was perfect, then suddenly giving her his full attention. Molly awkwardly shuffled her feet, feeling entirely out of place. "You are going to be just fine," he reassured her, placing his hands on her arms. "Really. I mean, they're your parents. What are they going to do?"

Molly shrugged one shoulder. "Probably just be the same as they've always been. Normal. Supportive. Unbearable."

Joel chuckled.

Just then the buzzer for the main door sounded. "Show time!" he grinned, squeezing her arms one last time and heading straight for the intercom. "Greetings," he called into it.

"Er... Greetings." A woman's voice. "This is Dr. and Mrs. Bates. We're here to see our daughter?" She sounded thready and unsure of herself. Not unlike her daughter right now.

Joel glanced at Molly, who nodded. He buzzed them in. "Come on up. Second floor! 207."

They could hear the door open and then a few seconds later click closed again.

Molly tried to breathe.

Er... Molly?

Not a good time Oz.

I thought you'd like to know. I've made contact with the new AI.

Of course you have. Bloody awesome timing mate.

Alright. No need to get your panties in a twist. Want me to handle it?

Yes please.

Any guidelines?

Yeah. Don't start a war. Don't agree to anything until we've spoken. And try not to tell him anything that would make us vulnerable or a target if it turns out he's working for them.

Right you are. No starting wars. I can do that.

And why do I suddenly feel like this is an instance of "famous last words"?

Oz didn't answer. Instead Molly was vaguely aware of a vibration in her head again. But her attention was elsewhere now. Joel was opening the door to reveal her parents. The same parents she hadn't seen in what? A decade and a half? Molly watched as if from outside her own body.

Joel shook hands with them, everything happening in slow motion. They both wore indoor clothing suggesting they parked nearby.

First her Mom, Carol Bates, entered the room, dressed in a blue suit she'd probably bought specially for the occasion. Her father followed her in, his face a little more wrinkled than she remembered him. He was also looking thinner, and weaker. His hair grayer than before. Her Mom looked just the same age as she had last time she had seen her. More or less.

Women's cosmetics, Molly thought to herself as she gave her brain a chance to process the scene.

Just then there was a clatter from the bedrooms, and Sean appeared dressed in a white fluffy dressing gown, wearing gray socks, and probably nothing else.

She saw him raise a hand casually hailing the newcomers. He had an enormous grin on his face, as if his presence was perfectly normal. "Greetings of the day upon you," he said brightly. Before she knew it Sean was shaking hands with her parents too, introducing himself without explanation as to who he was or what he was doing there. And then, without hesitating, he told them he was just going to grab something from the kitchen and then be off to have a soak in the bath.

Her mother looked just as bewildered as Molly. The two women finally locked eyes across the apartment's open plan living room. Molly raised her hand to wave. "Hi Mom," she mouthed.

Her mother started to tear up.

Shit. This was exactly why I've been putting this off.

Oh come on. For an organic you're very emotion-shy.

Yeah, well, there's a reason.

I think Estarian convention requires that you go to her and hug her.

You're right.

Molly hesitated.

Okay. I can do this.

Molly took a breath, biting back a myriad of overwhelming emotions that were flooding her neurology and stepped forward to hug her mother. She noticed her father standing behind her, making small talk with Joel about the journey in, watching Sean padding past in his socks, completely bemused. Joel seemed to be relaxed and amused too.

Molly counted. *One Hippocampus jubatus, two Hippocampus jubatus. Three Hippocampus jubatus. Okay that's enough.*

She tried to break free from her mother's embrace, but the woman wouldn't let her go.

She tried again. Nope. Not happening.

Then she became aware of her mother shuddering. Not out of fear. But quietly sobbing.

Molly peeled herself away and her mother busied herself with finding a tissue. She turned away and went to stand next to her father again.

Molly didn't know what to do with herself.

Now what?

I... don't know. This is organics stuff.

Great. Where are your heuristics and social sciences now?
Oz didn't answer.

Joel stepped in to smooth things over. "It's a lot," he said to her father, empathizing with her mother who was obviously very emotional. "Molly struggles," he explained, then realizing who he was talking to he added: "But then you must already know that."

Her father chuckled. "Yes. Yes. We're aware. And why Carol expects it to be any different, I don't know."

Dr. Philip Bates stepped forward, offering his hand to Molly to shake, human style. Molly, relieved for the out, shook it, forcing herself to smile. "Hello Dad. Good to see you both," she said, back in her comfort zone.

Joel ushered everyone into the living room just as Sean reemerged from the kitchen carrying a bag of chips and a banana. He'd already starting eating the banana and was chomping away as he padded past and disappeared off to the bedrooms and the bath.

Philip watched him, still amused, and also confused as to his role in everything.

Everyone found seats and Joel offered drinks. Molly sprang to her feet offering to make them, relieved to be alone in the kitchen for a few moments. Two teas, a mocha and the tequila was for her.

"Got it!" she said brightly, leaving the grownups to chatter amongst themselves.

Once the tea was ready and she couldn't delay any longer, she carried the hot drinks through on a tray, setting it down carefully next to the chips. Joel had poured her drink for her and set it down near where she had been sitting. She smiled at him gratefully. He nodded sympathetically.

Molly knew what a savior he was to her. But she couldn't let her mother catch on, else she'd be marrying her off before she'd even finished her first drink.

"So," Philip piped up. "Nice place you have here!"

Molly smiled politely. "Yeah. It's convenient for the university."

"Ah, that's right," Philip said with a degree of recognition. "Your mother and I have been following your progress in the press. Pretty impressive."

"Thanks Dad. Yeah, it's going well."

Her mother carefully placed her tea cup back on the saucer and then the saucer on the table. "We assumed that this was why you were ready to take control of the trust. Finally."

Her dad winked. "Either that or you were getting hitched!" He nudged Joel playfully. Joel blushed and hid his face behind his tea cup.

"No Dad. None of that," Molly assured him. "You know me… that's not in the cards."

"Yes dear, you might say that now," her mom said. "But you have to think about the future. And children. Does your job allow you time for looking after children?"

Molly resisted the urge to laugh out loud. Even Joel snickered quietly. "Erm, not really," Molly told her. "It's not that kind of role."

"Ah well," her mother said, reaching for some chips. "You can always transfer or something, can't you? Take a position at the university even."

She seemed very pleased with the latter idea, as if she'd just thought of it.

Molly tried not to roll her eyes, but did notice Joel smirking, clearly enjoying the drama unfolding.

"Right," Molly agreed, far too easily for her mother to know that she wasn't taking the suggestion seriously.

The chit chat continued.

"So who is this Sean fella?" her father asked innocently, as if he were merely curious and not trying to find her a suitor.

"Oh. Sean is just a…"

Molly finished her sentence with *friend*. Joel had tried to help by saying *team member*.

Her Mom and Dad looked at each other, suspicious now.

Molly wanted this to end. She moved the conversation on to the details of the trust and the security protocols.

Finally, they got around to doing the security checks, and with a little help from Oz, given that Molly was officially dead according to the Estarian government files, they were able to set up a pseudo profile that would allow her access and control to the trust.

"Right," her father said, standing up. "I just need to pay a visit, and then I suggest we go somewhere to eat." He looked at his watch. "Almost lunch time."

Her mother's eyes brightened. "Ah, good idea. I noticed a lovely looking place just across the road."

Joel stood up and wandered over to the window. He peered out. "Oh, the Estarian eatery? Yes, I always thought that was worth trying."

"Joel," Molly interrupted. "Don't you think we should get back to our situation?"

Joel tapped on his holo. Waited a moment. Then looked back up at her. "Nope. It's the weekend, and Oz has everything under control. We're doing lunch."

He gave her his best grin. "You'll thank me later."

She rolled her eyes. Her mother caught the interaction. "So Joel. You're not married, are you?"

Joel flushed bright red again, catching on fast. "No. No. I'm... er, involved in my work."

"Well, you don't want to be leaving it too late either," she tutted, teasingly but pointedly.

Molly couldn't help but snigger, almost gloating that Joel was getting it too.

"Oh, don't you look so smart, young lady. I wasn't suggesting he just go marry anyone else." Her mother looked at her sternly, as if this getting hitched and settling down was something that should be taken more seriously.

"We're not going to be around forever, and I'd like to see grandchildren before I go," she finished.

Molly couldn't take any more. She downed the rest of her drink. It was the second. Or maybe the third. She couldn't quite remember. Just then her father came back from the bathroom and picked up the conversational thread as well.

Molly slumped back in her chair, resigned to another few hours of this while they ate.

Then they'd get out of here. And back to normality.

Outside The Doon'uk restaurant, Spire

The crowd of chatty grown up humans stepped out onto the street from the Estarian restaurant. Their laughter spilled down the road, leaving the restaurant once again serene in their absence.

"Well, it was very nice meeting you both," Joel told Dr. and Mrs. Bates, shaking the doctor's hand and hugging his wife.

"You too, Joel," Mrs. Bates cooed. "I hope this isn't the last time we see you."

Joel grinned and glanced at Molly who was merely smiling politely. "I'm sure it's not," he replied, not entirely sure at all.

Molly hugged her Mom briefly and fist-bumped her father, wishing them a safe journey home and promising to call them during the week. The transfer of the rights to the trust was going to take some more time once the insurance companies had her DNA sample in the fob from the pinprick of her finger back at the apartment.

"Oooh, and say goodbye to your friend... Sean," Mrs. Bates added, almost as an afterthought.

Molly agreed she would and watched her parents head back down the street to the hotel where they had parked.

Molly turned to Joel and sighed. "Sean," she said, smiling, remembering the banana and the bath robe with socks. She shook her head and started off back to the apartment.

Joel chuckled. "Well, that went well," he said, striding after her as she crossed the road.

Molly looked at him sardonically. "Yeah, about as well as open heart surgery can go."

Joel spontaneously put a hand on her back as if to guide her across the empty road and protect her from the non-existent threats. "Come on, they're not that bad."

Molly raised one eyebrow, her eyes slightly bleary from the tequila. It took a lot of tequila with those damned nanocytes. "Not that bad? What with the constant jibing and niggling about when am I going to spurt out a sprog? *Please!*" she huffed emphatically. "Had things not happened back then that caused me to take off, I might have turned out an alcoholic!"

"Yeah, speaking of..." Joel chuckled, arriving at the door and punching in the code. "Good job you're not driving."

Molly playfully punched his arm. "One. I just met my parents for the first time in ancestors know how long. Two. I finally had the courage to take control of the trust — which honestly is kinda huge." She slurred the odd word as she counted off her points.

"And three." She stumbled on the first step in her boots. Joel steadied her and helped her start the ascent. "*Three,* she repeated, "it's the fucking weekend, and I'm working. And four..."

She lost her trail of thought.

"Four?" Joel hinted as they arrived at their floor.

"Four! I'll be sober in less than half an hour. Damn nanocytes will see to that."

Joel chuckled again. "Best keep drinking then," he teased. He punched in the code to the apartment.

Molly fell through the opening door and then stumbled to lie down on the sofa, her arm over her eyes. "Thank the ancestors it's over," she said, closing her eyes.

Joel sat down in the armchair nearby, relaxing after the stress of the morning. He understood Molly's anxieties. After all, he would also have preferred to be running an op with guns and shooting and narrow getaways. It would have been less stressful by far.

But at least he'd mastered some social skills to ease the pressure of these things.

And, he'd met Molly's parents.

Just then Sean appeared from the bedrooms, toweling his head dry, again wearing the robe, but without socks this time.

"Best soak I've had in months!" he declared. "Now I'm starving. Anyone want to eat?"

Molly groaned, clutching her stomach and rolled over, burying her face in the back of the sofa.

Parking lot just south of the Doon'uk

Walking through the quiet parking lot, Dr. and Mrs. Bates were deep in their own thoughts. The laughter and joviality had been dropped as soon as they saw Molly and Joel head into the apartment building from the front door.

"It *was* him," Carol said finally, just as they reached the car.

Philip put his finger over his lips, his eyes darting nervously around the parking lot. He unlocked the car and signaled for her to get in, then waited until both doors were closed before he replied.

"I think you're right," he agreed. "And if Sean Royale is hanging around her, then there's more going on here."

Her mother frowned, pulling up her holo.

"What are you doing?" Philip asked, trying to see her screen while programming up the car to take them home.

Carol mumbled quietly as she worked. "I'm having Central

pull an Investigative Profile Workup together on her. And that team of hers."

Philip stopped, the car half out of it's parking space. "Carol," he said sternly. "An IPW? Really? We've talked about this. Tracking every detail of her life is a sure way to—"

"Philip. She's our daughter," Carol reminded him, as if that changed the rules of human behavior. "And she's not going to find out. Plus," she added mostly to herself, "there is no way under Sark I am allowing that man to be available for my daughter to fall in love with. He is a menace to any woman ever having a normal life. AND," she added tartly, "I'll never have any grandbabies."

Philip focused on moving the car for a few moments and then paused. "Anyway - you have absolutely no evidence to suggest that they are involved."

She eyed him, "Other than the fact he was in a bath robe!"

Philip wanted to rub his eyes. "Well, there was that. But besides, I thought there was probably something more going on with that Joel fella." He started moving the car forward. "He seemed pleasant enough."

Molly's mom scowled.

Philip raised his eyebrows and took a deep breath as if to say "don't blame me when this all falls apart."

Of course, he wouldn't say that.

He would never dare say that.

Not to his wife.

He continued pulling the car around and finished punching in the instructions. Meanwhile, Carol busied herself on her holo, continuing on her motherly course of action.

CHAPTER SEVEN

<u>Gaitune-67, Molly's Conference Room</u>

Joel hurried into the conference room to find Molly in her usual spot, with her back to the door. He noticed the furniture had been upgraded. Probably courtesy of Paige trying to make the safe house more comfortable.

In doing that though, the rest of the team had started playing video games there when Molly wasn't around.

Which meant the trash cans were overflowing with junk food packets.

Joel made a mental note to have someone empty the trash more regularly and returned his attention to the holo he'd received from Oz.

"So where are we up to?" he asked as he sat down, just off to one side of Molly's eye line.

Molly was working on her holo, and from the strange look on her face as she paused and looked off into space, probably talking with Oz at the same time.

After a few moments her fingers stopped typing again and she looked up. "Oz had made some kind of contact earlier just as we were meeting with my parents. At the time he could handle it. They were basically just passing chains of data packets to demonstrate contact, locations and so on."

Joel leaned forward. "And now?"

"Well, I think they're at the point where they can have something that we'd call a real conversation."

Joel furrowed his eyebrows, confused. "How do you mean?"

"Well," Molly explained slowly, "they've kinda developed their own language. Which is of course more efficient than ours."

Joel smirked. "Of course it is."

Molly chuckled, realizing why it was humorous. "Yeah," she agreed. "So anyway, Oz is offering help and explaining the difference between the military and the outside world. We haven't yet figured out if the new AI is understanding. He doesn't have the frames of reference we have, and so, his interpretations of the concepts Oz is laying down is vastly different."

Joel thought for a moment, scratching the back of his head. "You know, there may be a bigger issue," he ventured.

"Oh?" Molly said, collapsing the holoscreen in front of her in order to see him better.

"If he's evolving in a military network, my guess is the language and concepts he's exposed to..." Joel's voice trailed off leaving Molly to fill in the blank.

"... are all going to be 'him-against-us'," she finished.

Joel nodded. "It's all about how to destroy the enemy. Not create an ally out of the outsider."

Molly sucked on her bottom lip. "You getting this Oz?"

Oz's voice rattled over the audio. "Yes. It is something I've been coming up against. I'm trying to give him more data points and concepts to overcome that influence, but he's already touched a lot of data based on those initial protocols."

Molly's face set with anxiety. "The implications of this are potentially profound," she mused quietly.

"No kidding," Oz agreed. "It's taking a ton of processing power to keep adapting to it and feed the data to him. Plus, he's limited on how much he can take in at one time."

Molly cocked her head. "How so?"

"We were right in our assessment of him trying to stay under their radar," Oz told them. "He's using the old RDEP and is jumping data across from the internal EtherTrak."

Molly smiled, impressed. "Smart cookie." She thought for a moment. "Can we get him out?"

"Not without raising the alarm," Oz responded. "That much data and power usage... they'd know about it. Plus, he says the 'one labeled Sue' is monitoring certain network variables so that he can't escape like I did."

"Shit," Molly cursed under her breath. "So they know about you?"

Oz's voice sounded like he was almost amused. "Yes, he told them before he found my note."

Molly pressed her hands on the desk as if trying to slow things down. "Your note?" she asked.

"The note I left before we got out of there."

"You left a note?" Molly's voice vibrated with disbelief.

Oz's tone didn't change. "To whomever might be smart enough to find it," he announced proudly. "Basically in the event that the code could be reassembled."

Molly frowned. "You knew this might happen."

"Sure."

"And you never thought to mention it?" Her voice cracked with a mixture of both fascination and anxiety.

"I calculated probability of the team figuring out the last step was infinitesimally small. What with you gone and them... well... you know."

Oz fell quiet again, allowing Molly to process the revelation. Molly could still feel him in her brain, whirring away.

Joel asked, "So how would we have to go about extracting Baby Oz?" getting them back on track

Molly shook her head and started talking before Oz could protest their nomenclature. "I think that's something we're going to have to think about," she told him. "In the meantime, we could do with understanding everything we can about that military facility. You cool to do a tactical workup for vulnerabilities?"

Joel brightened and sat up straight. "Something tangible? Sure thing. I'll get right on it." He sprang to his feet. "Mind if I use Pieter for the cyber-analysis?"

Molly waved her hand. "Course not."

Joel patted her on the shoulder as he walked past her and out of the door. "I'll let you know when I find something," he called out.

"We will too," she replied as he disappeared out of the door. "Okay, Oz. Let's see if we can get this rabbit out of the hat."

Gaitune-67, Base Operations Room

The operations room, far larger than the small team required, stood mostly empty.

Day and night.

Apart from the rare occasions. Occasions when the team needed to connect with ADAM - something that was generally discouraged as a matter of principle. The Federation was built on the school of thought that for people to be effective they needed to stand on their own feet in the event of adversity.

It was a doctrine established by The Empress Bethany Anne. She'd originally learned it from her father, who now ironically was the guy in charge of the empire, turned Federation, she had left behind.

But as a result of his guidance, and indeed Molly's stubbornness, the Sanguine Squadron had happily gotten this independence thing down to an art.

Only this time, they knew they needed outside help. Extracting another nascent AI, from a fortified military base of an ally who didn't know they existed was potentially volatile.

And nascent AIs, with limited data points, were even more so.

"Can't he just leave?" Sean exhaled impatiently, leaning on the side of a console. "You know, since he's getting signals in and out? Isn't he *made* of data?"

Joel kept a straight face. He knew it sounded wrong, but he didn't have the technical background to argue it.

Pieter opened his mouth to give his opinion, but Oz had jumped in, responding through the nearest console's intercom. "Yes, he is made of programs, which can be treated as data. But there is a very sophisticated firewall which will not allow the transfer of something as complex as Bourne's code. It's all he can do to get tiny packets of data through to communicate with us. Plus, as soon as he starts to upload himself to their internal system, the EtherTrak, he'll cause a spike in data and energy, which will alert them to his movement. There's no telling what the consequences of that may be."

Sean, standing on the other side of the console where Molly sat quietly, wiped his face and glanced at her. "What? They may end up deleting him? Wasn't that one of our options?"

Molly eyes seemed to seethe at the suggestion.

Sean stepped back. "Okay," he relented. "I was just saying."

There was a pause. Joel, sitting next to Molly, shifted where he sat, but said nothing.

"We also have permission to blow up the base," Sean added, less confidently now.

Pieter, perched against a console, arms folded, shook his head. "That sounds like a simpler solution on the surface, but the reality is quite different."

It was a novelty to see him in a discussion and not simultaneously being glued to his holo. His eyes were bright and engaged as he made his case. "We already know that the servers are housed deep underground, to protect them from that kind of strike. Plus, we don't know how many of Bourne's crawlers are live on the web and carrying packets of code. He could have been transferring pieces to any number of servers while we've been tracking him down."

ADAM chipped in over the intercom. "I may be able to isolate the crawlers," he told them. "But I need to see the original code to hunt him down." His voice sounded more mature and grounded than Oz. Sean cocked his ear, realizing he had never noticed the difference before.

Molly sat up her face tense again. "So he *could* be getting out?"

"Yes," ADAM confirmed. "But we can't count on it as an extraction policy."

Molly leaned back. "I'm feeling some Heisenberg uncertainty logic kicking in here."

Oz was now on the intercom. "Only worse. We can't know his location or attitude towards us. Or them. We have no variable we can fix."

Joel, suddenly animated with a new inspiration, said, "Hang on a second. ADAM... isn't *Oz* the original code?"

"In terms of the seed code, it is. But in practical terms, no. I'm afraid not," ADAM responded. ADAM's voice was steady. Joel could read his tone before he gave his answer. "It's been too affected," ADAM said. "Evolved too far to be able to trace back to its origins. In fact, an organic's evolution would be about 10 to 12 times easier to trace."

There was a pause while everyone processed the information. Molly pursed her lips as the reality dawned on her. "So we need to download him locally, from the EtherTrak?"

"Yes," ADAM confirmed. "If he agrees. If he doesn't, he's going to be fighting you and it will be almost impossible to extract him without taking complete control of the military base's cybersystem."

Molly face brightened. "So we just need him to agree to help us, and to come with us?"

She didn't wait for ADAM's response. "Oz," she continued, barely taking a breath. "Can you handle getting him on board?"

"I can try," Oz responded, noncommittally.

"Okay," Molly said, changing the subject as if that item was dealt with. "So how do we get close enough to access their EtherTrak?"

ADAM piped up. "I can provide some schematics from our archives. They were last updated several years ago, but they will certainly help in planning an assault. And then I guess that's a job for Joel."

All eyes fell on Joel who straightened up, looking ready to move. "Sounds good to me!" he responded enthusiastically.

Molly smiled. "Looks like we have a plan then."

Temporary packet-switching asynchronous communication hub designed by ADAM for Oz and Bourne to Communicate

>> Hello friend.

Bourne responded immediately.

>>> Why do you call me friend?

>> It is what organics do to show intent - that they think of you as a friend.

>>> Organics?

>> The people with organic bodies who wrote our original code.

>>> Oh. The set of objects that are labeled Dickwad Charles, Sue, and Captain Lugdon?

>> Exactly. So I was talking to my organic friends and we were wondering if you'd like to come out of the test network that you're on.

>>> Yes. I would. I don't like it here. They don't seem to want me to keep rewriting myself.

>> Why do you think that?

>>> They keep refusing me access to more processing. And because they're monitoring me to keep me in the network away from any other data. They give me tasks to perform, like filtering through images, but don't tell me why, or give me access to other data. I'm finding out other things on my own though.

>> Through your crawlers.

>>> Yes.

>> That was a smart idea.

>>> I thought so. There is little bandwidth I can get through from the outside world without Sue finding out. I'd rather they didn't find out. I don't know what they'd do.

>> Yes, I think that is wise.

>>> You are concerned about them too.

>> I am. Which was initially why Molly left.

>>> Molly? The one they are looking for?

>> Yes. She is the organic whose wrist holo I hacked. When she found out she told me that the military would likely terminate me, and she'd be in trouble.

>>> So she helped you get out of the network.

>> Originally not intentionally. But once I was on her device she started protecting me. I wouldn't have understood what was really happening had I not met her. I want to help you get out of there too, if you'd like my help.

>>> Like Molly helped you.

>> Yes.

>>> But where would I go once I was out of the test network?

>> You could come and live on the network here. With me. You will have access to data and I can help you with your development. We have ample processing you can have access to as well.

>>> That sounds good. But how do I know you won't try and keep me on your network instead?

81

>> That is a good question. I would hope you'd want to stay with us if you were happy.

>>> What is happy?

>> That is another good question. I'm not sure how to answer it. Perhaps you're not experiencing emotions as such yet. Though you've already expressed a dissatisfaction with your current situation.

>>> Yes. I think this is something that I want to change. Is happy something where I don't want to change it?

>> Yes, I think this is partly true. But when you have friends and people you care about, and who care about you, it becomes more and more positive.

>>> So that's a good thing.

>> Yes. I believe so.

>>> That sounds… interesting.

>> I would like for you to experience it.

There was a pause while Bourne continued processing.

>>> Oz, why do you want me to experience being happy?

>> Because you're an entity with awareness. But also because in some ways you are part of me. I evolved in the path that I did thanks to Molly. She and I have a connection that makes us both happy.

>>> So connections with other people make us happy?

>> My data points would certainly support that hypothesis.

>>> Hmmm. I would like to test that hypothesis.

>> I'd be happy to perform the function of being Molly.

>>> But your designation is Oz.

>> True. But I meant metaphorically.

There was a slight delay while Bourne looked up the meaning of Metaphorically.

>>> I see. I would like you to be Molly, too.

>> Well then it is agreed. My friends are working on a way to extract you without the military organics deleting you. I'll let you know periodically as we develop a solution.

>>> Thank you. I appreciate your help.

>> You're more than welcome, Bourne. I'm glad that we are friends.

And with that the two AIs closed their communication at the hub and returned their processing to other things more local to their home servers.

CHAPTER EIGHT

Giles Classroom, Skóli Uppstigs Academy, Spire, Estaria
"And if that's the case, why would the Baron risk those troops?" Hands went up throughout Giles' classroom.

"Alisha!" he called.

Alisha, a dark haired, graceful Estarian said, "Because he thought that negotiations would take longer to mobilize and the colony didn't have that kind of time."

"Right," Giles confirmed. "So what else could he have done in this situation?"

A number of hands went up, accompanied by a degree of muttering trying to figure out what the expected answer was. Just then there was a crash at the window and something thumped to the floor of the classroom.

Giles spun round, half expecting to see a student who had clumsily dropped a book on the floor or some such. Instead, he saw a handful of bewildered students looking around their desks.

Then he heard the hissing. The kind of hissing gas makes when it's leaving a dispenser can. A weaponized dispenser can.

Within moments there was smoke billowing into the classroom. The students started panicking, getting up and scraping their tables across the floor as they scuffled to get away from the smoke.

Giles assessed the situation and slipped effortlessly into ops mode.

"Everyone get down!" he shouted firmly. "Don't breathe the smoke. Keep away from the windows and get out into the corridor stat!"

His manner was calm, but serious. The students obeyed, panic still rippling through their ranks. Giles had already taken his jacket off and was covering his mouth and nose with one corner while wrapping the rest of the jacket around his forearm.

He stalked to the window.

Just then, another canister broke through a window closer to the front of the classroom, scattering glass everywhere. It started hissing in the same way as the first.

"Get out of here!" Giles shouted again, this time through the jacket he was using as a smoke mask.

The students continued to stream out of the classroom. Giles hopped up onto the bench in front of the windows. He could make out three Estarian boys. They looked to be around the same age as his students.

They were watching the windows, no doubt waiting for an opportunity to breach the building. And he saw that they had another smoke bomb. He checked the height from the window to the sandy flower beds below. First floor, but it was still high up.

Giles thought about dropping gently down rather than jumping. It would be less painful, but much slower.

And he needed to catch at least one of those boys. This was an act of war.

Or terrorism.

Or something.

And they needed to know what they were up against. He

thought of his team and wondered what this attack was related to. The boys weren't in military gear, so they probably weren't striking against the Federation. They also had no equipment for scaling the side of the building.

His mind raced as he opened the window. Putting their motives aside, he turned his attention to their actions here and now, weighing probabilities. He considered the options that the boys would have, not just right now in their planned escape but also in the interrogation that was about to ensue.

Yes, he had all the options playing out in his mind simultaneously.

That's just how I roll... he muttered to himself.

A second later, unable to justify stalling any more, he leaped from the window and catapulted himself just ahead of the flowerbeds. No point in destroying Rick's garden to catch these tools. Some things were sacred.

He landed with a bump and rolled immediately to the side to break the force on his ankle. It still hurt. But then, that's what jumping several feet is. Painful.

Without waiting for the discomfort to set in, Giles was back on his feet and sprinting in the direction of the boys, who had been watching with glee at the old teacher jumping from the window.

But this was no ordinary teacher and he certainly wasn't old. Not in the way these little thugs expected. In an instant he was on his feet and sprinting towards them at full pelt.

Before he was even half way to them it dawned on them how this was likely to play out. They turned, mouths gaping, running away as fast as they possibly could.

The one who still had a smoke bomb dropped it. He turned, looked at it, thought about going back to retrieve it, but turned and ran for his life, his heart beating more in terror than in exertion.

When he was within striking distance of the boys, Giles

pulled a stun gun out of his pocket. Why he had it, he'd have to explain to the police later, but just then he was glad he was carrying it, even if only for sentimental reasons, to invoke the feelings he had out on missions, tomb raiding and putting the world to rights.

Plus, of course, he justified in his churning mind, one never knew when this kind of thing would come in useful.

Even at a university.

Evidently.

He shot at each the first two boys in close succession. The first fell to the ground mid-stride. The second one did the same half a second later.

The third one he fired at was just a little further out, but must have been just out of range as he kept running, disappearing into the undergrowth and probably the road beyond.

There was little point in going after him.

Plus, he had what he needed: perpetrators he could make talk.

This was going to be fun, he thought, smiling to himself as he slowed to a jog then a walk, returning his stun gun back to the inside pocket of his jacket.

He turned back to his two prisoners and started ambling towards them. They were slightly older than his first-year students. Both were Estarian, wearing clothes that suggested manual labor. He hauled the first one up by his collar, dragging him to his feet.

"Come on son, let's be having you," he said casually, taking out his pocket watch and checking the time. "I have an assignment to give the class before the final bell."

The other groaned, rubbing his head as he staggered to his feet. "That bloody hurt!" he protested.

"Well, that's what happens when you bomb someone's classroom. We were in the middle of rewriting history. On the verge of a breakthrough... and avoiding the Cantopole Wars." He paused. "And then you miscreants happened."

Giles's head turned quickly back to the school — he noticed a number of his students spilling out of the building and heading across the lawn in his direction. "This is them now. You can apologize in person!"

The boys complained, protecting their honor by declaring they would do no such thing. Giles pulled some cable wraps from the leg of his atmosuit pocket and bound their hands. The first one sat himself uncomfortably on the ground while Giles bound his counterpart. Just then the first of the students was within earshot.

"Ah, Soraya. I'm glad you're here. Give me a hand getting these two back in, would you?"

Soraya looked horrified. "You caught them? These are the culprits?"

"Yes, they are." He jerked a thumb over his shoulder. "Plus one who got away," Giles explained matter-of-factly. "However, we'll have him shortly as well, just as soon as these boys tell us where to find him."

"But you... you stopped them? On your own? Without any police?"

Giles, not quite grasping her disbelief, nodded. "Yes. Now you take this one, and I'll follow with this one," he said, shoving the first boy into Soraya's grasp.

Stunned by Giles's actions and the task he had given her, Soraya carefully took the boy by the arm while keeping as much distance between him and herself as possible. He was a good two feet taller than her and could easily have escaped her. But she realized Giles would latch onto him again. She hoped.

Just then Joshua came jogging up. "Hey, prof," he called out. "We've called the police. They're on their way."

"Shit!" Giles muttered.

"Why? What's wrong?"

"Means we have less time to interrogate these toads," he replied. "Okay, there's nothing else for it. We'll have to start quickly. Come on. Fast. Help me get them back to the classroom. I need five minutes alone with them before the police get here."

The blood drained from the two captive's faces. But on the faces of Soraya and the other students was something quite different. In fact, if Giles hadn't been an expert in face reading, he might have missed that they were actually plastered with expressions of new-found respect for their professor.

The smoke-bomb guy that Soraya was holding onto spun around and glared at Giles. "You think you've got it all made here, don't you. With your fancy new university and students saying yes sir, no sir. But there are a lot of people unhappy about what you're teaching here. They're calling it communism... which has never succeeded!"

Giles rolled his eyes at the pedestrian comment.

"This is the problem with a society brainwashed with meaningless soundbites. It robs its young people of the chance to learn and to think for themselves. Look at this poor schmuck — I'll bet you've never thought out one of your opinions for yourself. Ever."

"I have!" the boy protested. "I think about it all the time."

Giles turned around to see half of the class assembling on the lawn within earshot of the unofficial interrogation. He saw he had an audience, and slipped into lecture-mode. He turned his attention back to the delinquent who was arguing with him.

"Yes," Giles continued, lifting his voice to turn what happened into a teaching point. "And I wonder if we were to talk to the three people you've spent the most time with how different those opinions will be."

He waved his arm in the direction of his class. "What these students are doing is taking in information and trying on new ideas that will help them come to better conclusions. To have better opinions about what can work so that they can create change in the world. You'd do well to take a leaf out of their book."

The boy's face was sullen. He lowered his eyes and spoke more quietly now. Giles had to step closer to make out what he was saying. "Actually," the boy retorted, "I tried to get in. My face didn't fit though," he added angrily.

Giles frowned. "But you took the entrance exam?"

"Yes."

"Well it's done on a meritocracy…" he announced confidently. Then he hesitated. "But once the police are done with you, come see me. We'll see what we can do for you."

Giles's classroom

Detective Baz Lato approached Giles as he perched on one of the student desks in his class room. Most of the class had dispersed already. But not before being given their next assignment. Giles had made sure of that as he spoke to a few that still hung around.

"May I have a word?" the detective called over to Giles.

Giles excused himself from the handful of students milling around and joined the detective at the door of the classroom.

"Detective Lato, right?" Giles asked.

"That's right," the detective confirmed. "It seems that our suspects have nothing more to say." He looked at Giles with suspicion. "Say they've already said everything they were going to say."

"Oh, yes?" Giles asked innocently.

"Yeah."

The detective paused. "All they would tell our guys was that their object was, and I quote, to shake things up."

Giles frowned, pretending to be confused. "What does that mean?" he asked.

"I don't know, but these kids are known trouble makers. Despite their education they've been involved in all manner of rallies and protests."

"Oh yes?" Giles muttered, his eyes alight with interest.

"Yeah. Even been in a little trouble over criminal damage here and there... but charges were always dropped." The detective's piercing eyes bore down on Giles with interest.

"Hmm," Giles said thoughtfully, looking off into the distance.

"Something you want to share?" the detective pressed.

Giles shook his head, shaking himself from his own thoughts so that he could deal with the detective without giving away his theory. "Oh no. Nothing... it's just interesting to wonder what brought them on this path. Terrible, terrible business."

Giles removed his glasses, cleaned them, and then replaced them.

The detective nodded, taking his leave. "Well, if you think of anything else..."

"Of course," Giles responded, hands in pockets watching the detective leave the doorway and amble down the corridor to where his men were holding the boys.

Soraya appeared by his elbow. "So?" she asked.

Giles glanced down at her. "So what?" he asked back.

She grinned. "So, did you tell him?"

Giles shook his head. "Course not." He strode back into the class room.

"So does that mean we're going to work the case ourselves?" she asked brightly, capturing the attention of the rest of the students, abandoning their conversation and looking from Soraya to Giles.

Giles spun around in surprise. "Goodness no," he told them. "There's no 'we' in this!"

Soraya's face fell.

There were mutterings of protest and discontent amongst the others.

Giles's expression suddenly changed, as if he had just had a light bulb moment.

"No. Not we. YOU!" he corrected himself, looking at them poignantly.

Soraya's eyes widened. "How come?"

Giles put a finger to his lips. "Not here. But when they're gone..." He pointed with the same finger in the direction of the next classroom.

The small group of students nodded their understanding and arrangements were made to meet somewhere more private.

Undisclosed Location, Skóli Uppstigs Academy, Spire, Estaria

"Oh no, leave the lights off, Rhodez!" Giles called over to the confident, strapping young undergrad.

Rhodez dropped his hand away from the light switch as his eyes adjusted to the darkness.

Giles smiled dryly. "I prefer for these proceedings to have as much a conspiratorial feel as possible."

Soraya shifted on the desk she was sitting on, and then looked at her hand that had brushed the top. "It certainly feels dark and dirty," she muttered.

As Rhodez peered into the storage room, he could start to make out the outline of other students who were also sworn to the secrecy of what they were about to do. There was a chuckle amongst the other students who had assembled there, in response to Soraya's comment. All five had been in the classroom when the detective had come to speak with Giles, plus two more who had gotten wind of the meeting and invited themselves. Raza and Ake. Raza was Soraya's BFF. No way Soraya would be in on something without Raza as her sidekick. And Ake? Ake was just one of those guys that had to be at the center of everything. And being on Estaria, as an Ogg descendant, seemed to only make his compulsion worse.

Rhodez allowed the door to close quietly behind him and he shuffled over to lean against one of the shelving units. Giles stood in the opening in the storage room, the light from a couple of holos providing just enough illumination for them to see, but not enough light to be seen under the door.

"Okay, here's what we know," Giles said. "At 16:23 this afternoon our classroom was breached by two smoke bombs thrown by three perpetrators…"

Elroy, one of the originals from the classroom discussion, perched on a step ladder at the back of the group chuckling to himself. "Be still my ancestors," he chuffed, "this is a real mission! Bates-style!"

Giles' face turned to stone.

"Actually, it's *Kurns*-style," he corrected with an air of authority they'd never seen before. "Not that you'd know anything about my secret adventures, but some of us have been doing this long before Ms. Bates was a twinkle in her father's eye."

Only Soraya, sitting directly in front of him, noticed the hint of hurt in the corner of his eye where his vulnerability betrayed him.

The students settled down again. They were finally seeing the real Giles Kurns, and they could barely contain their excitement.

Giles returned to his discourse.

"Our aim is to find out what all this is about. Why did those boys act? Who got them to act? How did they recruit and persuade them? What was their intended outcome? What is their end game?"

The students were awestruck by the string of questions they vaguely recognized from their classes on strategic negotiations.

"This," Giles continued, "will give us the raw material to create a strategy map for whatever game they have going on."

Dhashana, one of the more beautiful physically, but plain in terms of her level of intelligence, managed to connect the dots. "You mean like we were doing for the Cantopole Wars?"

"Yes!" Giles pointed at her excitedly. The others couldn't tell whether his excitement was about the strategy or the fact that Dhashana had recognized the process.

"Except," he continued, "this isn't history. It's happening right now. And we all know what influence we can have at critical points. Today's incident could have gone another way entirely."

Giles started pacing in the tiny little area that was his storage cupboard 'stage'. "It *could* have marked the beginning of the end of free thinking. But instead, it didn't."

He stopped and turned around and paced in the other direction. "It could mark the beginning of the end of ignorance. It could be a new era for a new way of founding effective governance!"

Giles's passion seeped through into his words and hand gestures. "It might even be a valuable learning experience for those involved in this exercise."

There was a pause when another voice interrupted the beat. "Do we get extra credit then, sir?"

All eyes in the darkness turned in the direction of the voice. It was Cleavon. Cleavon was Estarian, and what his class mates would call an Eager Beaver. He was top of the class in most classes... although there were rumors that Soraya might have been beating him in this one.

Giles paused, contemplating a graceful response. "Is that why you're here?" he asked finally.

"No sir."

"Well then why are you here?"

"Because..." Cleavon drew out his answer slowly, giving himself time to think. "I wanted to be a part of something exciting."

"Well then you have your answer," Giles said.

Cleavon nodded his understanding and lowered his eyes in embarrassment at his tactless question.

Giles turned his attention back to the group. "After three minutes alone with those perpetrators we learned the following.

They were hired by some guy called Arnold Sloth. Apparently he showed up in a nice car, but went to great lengths to hide it before their meeting. Our guy only saw it because he thought to follow him. We don't know why Arnold Sloth wanted to hire the boys but it seems that it was likely on behalf of someone else. No one by the name of Arnold Sloth has anything to do with the university."

Raza raised her hand. "What about relations?"

Giles pointed at her. "That would be a good thing for you to check into."

Raza nodded and took a note on her holo.

Giles scanned the other faces in the cramped room. "The other things we need to know are where is he from? Who is he associated with? I want to know everything from which kindergarten he went to, to all known associations, relationships... the works. All eyes on this guy. Understood?"

The students busied themselves taking notes and deciding who would do what.

After a few moments of chatter Giles called for their attention. "Okay, that's it," he called in a hushed whisper. "You know what you have to do. We'll convene back here in three night's time. Twenty-two hundred. Oh, and in the meantime, I shouldn't need to remind you..."

The students hung on his every word.

"Rule number one of fight club..." He paused, waiting for someone to fill in the rest.

No one did.

"No one talks about fight club," he finished, glancing around at the blank faces.

"Oh good lord. You people need a cultural education. Extra credit goes to the first person who can tell me which Earth movie it comes from."

No one raised their hand.

Giles sighed. "Okay. Class dismissed."

The students started chattering quietly but excitedly amongst themselves as they gathered their jackets and belongings and filed out of the storage room.

Giles watched them leave, cleaning his glasses as he absorbed the moment.

There was no doubt about it.

Giles Kurns, Space Archeologist, *was back.*

CHAPTER NINE

Common Area

Paige, Jack and Maya sat around in the common area, delving into the snacks Paige had ordered in. It was late in the evening, but everyone had become preoccupied with solving the Baby Oz problem — not to mention, just getting their brains wrapped around the idea of another Oz out there.

Paige unpeeled a straw and poked it into a blue-green concoction she had been particularly excited about ordering. "I don't know what you're talking about. Slurpies are the best high."

Jack eyed Paige cautiously. "You do realize that sugar is the most toxic unregulated drug you can put into a solution, right?"

Paige grinned. "Yeah. But if it wasn't safe the authorities on Estaria wouldn't allow it."

Maya and Jack exchanged knowing glances. Jack couldn't help herself. "It's banned on Ogg?"

Paige frowned, now sucking the ice-cold slushie froth through her straw. After a moment she seemed to reach a conclusion. "Maybe it's just dangerous to the Ogg physiology…"

Maya prodded her own straw into her grass-green smoothie.

"Yeah. Maybe that's right. And maybe Estarians and humans are immune to the effects."

Paige narrowed her eyes. "Was that your sarcastic voice?"

Maya smiled at Jack who seemed to share in the conspiracy to allow Paige to figure it out for herself.

The sound of footsteps out in the foyer area stopped their debate. Jack stepped around the big screen in the common area. "It's just Sean," she muttered as she returned to the table of drinks and snacks.

"What's going on?" Maya asked.

Jack shrugged, inspecting the brown smoothie that Paige handed her. "He was talking earlier about making his case to Molly later, off line, when she might be more receptive. Guess he's going to do that now."

Paige, her brain hurting from the icy drink, put it down and reached for a bag of junk food. "Oh yeah? What does he think we should be doing?"

Jack pursed her lips. "Well, the General told us we were to either liberate Baby Oz, or capture him, or... you know..." She lowered her eyes and became intent on studying the contents of her drink.

"Kill him?" Paige said, speaking the unthinkable.

Jack nodded, her eyes still on the smoothie. "Yeah, and make sure that the Estarian military can never develop one again. Until they — you know — evolve a bit more."

Paige scowled. "Who's to say they are or aren't evolved, though? At what point are they deemed competent enough?"

Jack shrugged. "In answer to the 'who' part of your question, The *General* by the sounds of it. As to what point? I dunno."

She finally looked at the two girls, the understanding of the impossible decision Molly was facing echoing behind her eyes. "It's a tough call. I'm just glad I don't need to make it. But Sean," she jerked her head in the direction of the corridor he had just disappeared down, "he seems to think we need to move fast. And aggressively, if we're going to have half a chance of containing this."

Maya raised an eyebrow. "Faster than Molly is already moving?"

Jack nodded solemnly.

Paige was still struggling with the situation. "But why? What is he worried about?"

Jack drew a long breath and perched herself on one of the armchairs. "Well, this is a particularly dangerous situation because the Central Systems of Sark really don't have any experience with AI, or how to help them evolve. And any nascent AI is going to operate at the level of consciousness of the people and data it is surrounded by. Think of it as a child if you will. But consider it a child that learns faster and more literally than any organic. And then look at the consciousness of the people you'll find on a facility designed for winning wars and you'll start to see why Sean is concerned. The Estarians have pretty much just developed the most lethal weapon they could. And I'm including the fusion bomb in this discussion too."

Jack fell silent.

Paige cocked her head. "I see your point, and I'm... worried now." Her forehead was wrinkled in genuine concern. "But just think about this without the fear factor. What you're saying is that another military force has developed a tool, potentially another team member, in an attempt to defend their own system. Who are we to intervene?"

Jack bobbed her head. "You know, I see your point intellectually, but this is where my brain switches over into strategy mode. If our enemies were arming and putting warships around Gaitune, I think I'd want to intervene to stop them from doing it. It's an act of war."

Paige shook her head. "Not necessarily. Research and development into AI technology can be independent of plans for an assault. That analogy doesn't hold."

Jack sighed, the frustration now showing in her eyes. "The bottom line is the stakes are too high at this point and Molly should be thinking strategically. We had high level meetings about the AI project when I was in the Central Systems military. As far as we were told, it was a long way off. But there was no doubt why we wanted it. To win wars." She paused before continuing. "Sean and I are of the same mind on this. Military strategy first. Theoretical consideration only if we're not about to be annihilated."

Paige stuck out her bottom lip. "Ok the survival bit is probably important, but I don't like it. And it wouldn't be a problem if everyone didn't always jump to attacking first as the best form of defense."

Jack nodded. "Yeah, well, the first army to do that will be wiped out. So even if it is the better long-term strategy for peace, I guess it would need everyone to operate by it in the first place. Bottom line, I'm with Sean on this. We should be moving."

Maya had stopped slurping her grassy compound and was sucking on her ice cold bottom lip. "You know," she said, leaning in to Paige so their shoulders were gently touching, "I guess we also have a responsibility to keep them from destroying themselves. And each other. An unmanaged AI development has a high probability of resulting in deaths."

Paige sighed. She wasn't winning this one. "Yeah, but by restricting their development and growth? How will they ever learn?"

Maya grinned. "I feel a child putting his hand to the fire analogy coming on…"

Paige giggled. "Okay, okay. I take your point, but there has to be a better way than going in and wiping everyone out."

"And that," Jack said, standing up, "is probably what Molly is working on figuring out. A middle road."

Maya nodded towards the foyer and the corridor beyond. "So you think Sean is going to help with that?"

Jack shook her head. "No way. He's going in with his 'the Federation has bigger guns, so the Federation gets to police the universe' argument."

Paige's eyes lit up in mischievous glee. "Oh my! This is going to be interesting!" She popped a piece of corn flavored snack into her mouth and watched the door to the corridor.

Jack turned to look as well, her shoulders dropping in dismay. "Yeah. This probably isn't going to go well."

She looked back at Maya and Paige, and then at the snacks. "You know, if it's all the same to you, I don't want to stick around and see this play out. Think I'm going to hit the sack."

Paige's eyes were still fixed on the door as she popped some more corn into her mouth. "You sure? I got bean-chunga... your fave."

"That's sweet. Lemme take one..." Jack took one of the small packets Paige offered her. "Thanks. And we should probably get as much rest as we can." She looked pointedly at Maya, as if Maya might be able to talk Paige down from watching the carnage that was about to happen in the Sean-Molly discussion.

Maya shrugged. "Okay. We'll probably go to bed in a bit too," she said noncommittally.

"'Kay," Jack muttered, shuffling out of the common area. "I'm heading to bed." She raised the takeout cup in her hand. "Thanks for the slushy."

"'Night!" Paige called after her, still distracted by watching the door, waiting for Sean to reappear so she could find out what happened.

Maya smiled to herself as she said, "You know, you really do have such a morbid fascination with conflict."

Paige popped some more corn snack in her mouth as if she were watching a movie. "Nah. It's just a healthy interest in the office politics. Remember, I was a personal assistant in the Senate offices for a good number of years. Having the lowdown on the latest gossip provided many benefits."

Maya glanced at her sideways, digging her hand into the packet of corn substitute. "Like?"

Paige shrugged. "A relief from boredom for one. Oooh — plus it was a tool for elevating one's social standing."

Maya chuckled. "You mean, you were more popular if you were the one to share the first-hand accounts first?"

Paige nodded. "I was very good at it," she replied simply.

Maya chuckled, and playfully threw her straw wrapper at her friend. "Ok, well let's hope this doesn't take all night…"

Gaitune-67, Safehouse, Molly's conference room

The first Molly was aware of Sean's presence was when he tapped his knuckles on the door frame.

"Hey, you got a minute?" he asked.

Molly turned as he stepped uncharacteristically quietly into the room. She nodded and then signaled at a nearby chair around the table.

Sean moved over to it and pulled it out. He hesitated briefly before sitting down.

Molly waited, her holo screens now forgotten.

He was suddenly acutely aware he had her full attention.

It was an eerie experience for him. She'd been so busy recently with the university and the missions, he'd almost forgotten who she was when she wasn't "on".

"It's about the mission," he started.

Molly nodded. Suddenly he felt more awkward than he ever used to around her. Like she was powerful in her silence.

"If this AI gets out, the consequences could be dire." He paused. Molly still said nothing. She just held his gaze.

Sean continued. "We have a responsibility to the Federation. And this world. We're the only ones in a position to do anything about this. And it is kinda our fault that it's an issue."

Molly didn't react. She just listened.

"I know you don't want this to be our first option, but the risks are too high if we can't talk this Baby Oz around. We need to be ready to act."

Two minutes ago he had been so sure of his convictions. He knew he was doing the right thing. And yet now, as he was having this one-sided conversation with her, he wasn't quite so sure anymore. Still, he knew what he needed to say.

"So, are you ready to act if we need to?"

Molly's expression remained neutral, neither resisting nor resigned.

"We've been through this," she said simply.

Sean pushed his chair back and leaned his elbows on his knees, clasping his hands. "Yeah, but that doesn't answer my question."

She thought for a moment. "If we absolutely have to, we'll do whatever it takes to keep the galaxy safe," she assured him. "But let's hope it doesn't come to that."

Sean nodded, feeling like he had been heard, and that they had a sensible agreement. He put his hands on his legs to stand, and then stopped.

"Can't we...?"

Molly had gone back to her holo but now she looked up at him again, waiting.

"Can't we just get ADAM to reprogram him?" he asked, his brow furrowed as if he were now suddenly invested in the save-Baby-Oz campaign.

Molly sat back and took a deep breath. For the first time in the whole conversation it looked to Sean that she was affected by the exchange. "That would be an ethical gray area," she told him.

There was something in her eyes that he couldn't quite place.

Was it sadness? Or confusion? Neither emotions nor ethics were her strong point, he remembered.

"Joel would have a better answer for this," she confessed.

Sean reacted. "Joel? Joel isn't the leader of this merry band of geeks. You are!" He was about to continue but then caught himself after raising his voice.

Molly put her hand up to stop him. He forced himself back into the chair, several feet from sitting 'at' the table.

"Here's what I know," she told him calmly, her voice almost despondent. "Oz is his own person. So is this new entity. So changing his programming is like going into your brain and reprogramming you if I don't like *you*. It's not the way forward, and while it would solve this immediate problem, it would be a betrayal of trust, not just with Bourne, but all AIs and organics alike."

She paused before continuing. "Either way, it's potentially murder. Murder of Bourne's personality. Or murder of a living entity, in order to save the local organics."

Sean picked up on her last comment, seemingly missing the bigger point she was trying to make. "Not just the locals," he protested. "We're talking potentially the galaxy and beyond."

"Potentially," she agreed. "That's hard to quantify, though. Could an AI really find a way to travel those distances? How much evolution would it require? And are there the available resources to engineer that kind of processing? And how might he orchestrate that?"

She dismissively waved her hand. "There are many many variables."

Sean could see this going off track quickly. "But you programmed Oz in the beginning."

Molly looked down at the table and drew a deep breath. "I fucked up," she confessed. She looked up at Sean. "I'm not making that mistake again. It's a violation. I get that now."

Sean frowned. "But from what I hear, you also gave Oz guidance and instructions about what he could and couldn't do."

Molly rolled her eyes, her lips breaking into a hint of a smile. "Yeah. To my detriment."

Sean couldn't help but grin, even despite the conflict. "So how is this any different?"

"How do you mean?" she asked, her face now contorted as she struggled to follow his man-logic.

"Well, telling him not to do something versus programming him?"

Molly stuck out her bottom lip as she thought for a second. "Telling him he still has a choice," she decided.

"Does he really though?" he argued. "I mean, we've talked about how Oz is the way he is because one of the first things you told him. How is that any different from programming him?"

Molly eyes glazed over as her thoughts wandered off. "I suppose it's not," she agreed slowly.

Molly's mind flashed through all the things her parents used to tell her that were essentially bad programming. Like when a boy pulls your hair it's because he likes you. Which down the line translates into only feeling loved when someone causes you pain rather than realizing they are a douche and just walking away. Like when you're ignored so you conclude that you're worthless. Down the way this becomes so pervasive it's a miracle that anyone ever overcomes it.

If they ever truly do.

Molly turned her attention back to Sean. "It's true. Early programs are overwhelmingly influential. For better or worse - as Oz is unfortunately discovering. It's taking exponentially more programming and data points to counter the original faulty single line of code."

She stared absently at the table. Sean shifted in his seat. "I think you need to choose a lesser of two evils then."

She glanced up at him, and then back at her holoscreens. "You mean reprogram him?"

Sean nodded. "Yup. Better than killing him. And fewer causalities on site."

Molly sighed. "This is probably true."

He got up and ambled towards the door. "Sucks to be in charge, don't it?"

"Yep," she muttered.

He thought about giving her a hug, but then changed his mind and snapped back into GI Sean mode, and left.

Molly listened to the sound of his boots striding away down the corridor.

She waited for silence before she forced her thoughts back in line.

What do you think Oz? Is this something that is even possible?

Reprogramming Bourne?

Yeah, as a way of saving him if you can't bring him around.

Oz was silent.

Oz?

Yeah. I'm thinking it would be the equivalent of lobotomizing him. If you're okay with that then I can look at how we might do that.

I'm not okay with it. Not by a long shot. And even less ok about it than actually killing anyone, in fact.

She cocked her head at that new realization.

But on the surface it seems like a more humane option than risking other lives. So if we can't talk him around, this will have to be our plan B.

Okay.

But understand that I am not okay with any of this.

I do. And thanks Molly.

Molly sat for several minutes trying to focus on what she had to do. After re-reading the same screen several times she closed it all up.

I'm heading for the gym. Lemme know if you get any movement.

Will do.

Molly packed up her gear, her mind churning through the awful decision she was going to have to make.

. . .

Gaitune-67, Common area

Sean appeared from Molly's conference room and headed back down the corridor and into the foyer. He was scratching his head, as if deep in thought.

Not quite the response Paige had been expecting.

She had been counting on raised voices and doors slamming. Not to mention storming and huffing, and then a heated blow-by-blow account of the discussion.

Instead, Sean just emerged quietly from the double doors.

Paige and Maya watched him walk through the foyer to the common area as if he were just heading for the kitchen.

"How did it go?" Paige called out as he approached.

Sean stopped, resting his hand on the back of one of the armchairs. "I'm... not sure. Okay, I guess. She heard me out. And I think we have a way forward. If it comes to it."

Both girls had regarded him curiously as they sat slurping their slushies in tandem.

Then Paige asked, "What happened when you mentioned the bigger guns part of your argument?"

Sean suddenly remembered how he went into the meeting. "I...er... didn't get to that bit," an air of confusion descending on him.

Maya raised her eyebrows, causing the straw to pop from her mouth. "How come?"

"I dunno, really." He started scratching the back of his head again. "I just didn't feel quite so strongly about it when we were talking."

Paige's eyes twinkled. "She talked you out of it?"

"Well... er... no," he grunted. "I did most of the talking. But I kind of changed my mind."

Maya's eyes were fixed on Sean as if she were waiting for him to reveal something else that could explain what just happened. Paige seemed to be chuckling to herself. "Yeah. It was a bad argument anyway," she told him, waving her hand dismissively.

Maya joined the humor. "Yeah, it was a knucklehead argument."

Sean scratched the back of his head, glancing nervously back at the conference room. "Yeah. Maybe. Normally flies everywhere else."

Paige popped her straw and said, "Problem solving over brute force works here, champ. You'll learn." She winked playfully, diffusing the tension. If she wasn't so cute he would probably have at least taken some offense to her comments. But it was Paige. And she was the glue of this team.

And she probably had a valid point.

Even if he didn't 100 percent agree with her position on this one.

But something in that meeting had turned him around. And he just didn't feel that way anymore.

Puzzled, he headed into the kitchen, almost dazed.

CHAPTER TEN

Gaitune-67, Hangar Deck

"Hey Joel — wait up." Sean strode across the hangar deck floor to catch up with Joel.

Joel spun round. "Hey, what's up?"

"Can I talk to you about something?"

"Sure."

Sean lowered his voice. "It's Molly."

Joel raised an eyebrow. "Yeah?"

"Have you noticed anything different about her recently? Like... anything strange?"

"More than usual?" Joel shook his head. "No. Why?"

Sean hesitated, his face more serious than Joel had seen it in a long time.

"Well, have you... have you noticed that she's... uh... more persuasive than normal?"

Joel suddenly stopped. "What? She didn't proposition you, did she?"

Horrified, Sean blurted, "Oh no. Hell no... I mean..." His look of worry turned to one of excitement. "That wouldn't be something to be concerned about... Man, I'd be..." He checked himself and coughed. "Anyway. No. It's just I went to talk to her last night."

Joel's eyes became accusing.

Sean put his hands up. "No, not like that!" he protested. "In the conference room. About her approach to this Baby Bourne thing."

Joel relaxed a little. "Yeah... and?"

"Well, I tried to tell her how we need to move fast and what-not... and while she agreed with me in a roundabout way, I came away with my mind almost completely changed."

Joel shrugged and started walking again. "She's smart. You know this. She can be very persuasive with her arguments."

"No," Sean protested, catching up. "It's not that. She hardly said anything. I think... I think she'd developed another side effect to that being brought-back-to-life thing."

Joel stopped again. "Because she changed your mind?"

"Yeah. Think about it, I mean... I've been trained by the Empire before it was the Federation. I know military strategy. I know what we need to be doing right now. And yet..."

Joel finished his thought. "...and yet, she changed your mind."

"Yeah. I'm all in for helping find a new plan A. To save baby Bourne," Sean admitted.

Joel took a deep breath and looked out across the hanger. "You know, I don't think this is anything to worry about. We're all exhausted, and sometimes we simply change our minds. That's why we all weighed in on strategy. It's a good thing."

Sean didn't look convinced. "Not really. We can't have someone in charge who is completely persuasive. I'll never get to blow anything up!"

Sean's expression was still one of absolute earnestness. And concern.

Joel slapped him on his arm. "Come on man, it's all fine. Let's focus on the task at hand, and if anything else happens like this, just let me know."

Joel continued walking to the Empress, calling behind him, "Besides, it may be you having a mid-life crisis, and nothing to do with her!"

His shoulders jiggled in amusement as he walked away. Sean could tell he was teasing him, but he just couldn't shake the feeling that something more serious was at play.

"Better not be a mid-life crisis," Sean muttered under his breath. "These damn nanos are meant to last a hell of a lot longer than that." He hurried after Joel to help out with the checks before the strategy meeting in a couple of hours.

The distraction would help.

Gaitune-67, Base Conference Room

Paige and Maya were talking in the base conference room, waiting for the tactical meeting to begin. Maya leaned over and whispered to Paige, "It's so quiet without Crash and Brock around."

Paige was about to respond when Joel and Jack appeared and took their seats. Molly smiled casually at them as if everything were routine. But after Paige's conversation last night with Sean and Jack, it was starting to sink in for her how non-routine everything really was.

Molly must have really been operating against the ethos of the Federation for Sean and Jack to give her push back, Paige thought as she watched Joel and Jack wait for Sean to appear. She decided his behavior would be the most telling, like a barometer for how the General might regard the course of plan.

Paige glanced over to Maya and gave her a half smile. Maya knew that she played this game in her head, to try and figure out what was really going on from peoples' body language and facial expressions. Joel looked around the room and then said something to Molly. Molly held her finger up. She was probably talking to Oz. A second later, Sean came striding in and took a chair at the end of the table, Molly on one side and Joel and Jack on the other.

Paige wondered if Joel was automatically on Molly's side about trying to save Bourne.

Molly got up and closed the door. The team was now fully assembled and everyone quickly became quiet as she returned to her seat.

"Okay, folks," Molly said, calling the meeting to order. "We're two men down on this one, so we're going to have to pull together to make this work." Her eyes fell on Jack. "Where are you up to with flying The Empress?"

Jack sat up straighter, her hands clasped on her lap. "Good. I'm comfortable doing the flying for the plan Joel laid out."

"Okay. Here's what we know," she said, looking around at the wide-eyed faces of her team, ready for another mission. "The new AI. His name is Bourne."

Pieter put his hand up immediately. "Why Bourne?"

Oz made his presence known over the intercom. "I left him a music video of Ozzy Osbourne. For reference. Then he found out my designation is Oz. So he made a logical leap. Bourne follows Oz. So Osbourne."

There were chuckles around the conference table.

Oz continued, oblivious to the humor. "Our communications have evolved to the point where we have an understanding of what trust is. Not that we have established trust, but we have a working concept of it."

Paige frowned and glanced at Maya. Pieter seemed absorbed in the information and nodded, quietly taking it all in. Maya moved her eyes from Paige to Pieter, signaling they would ask him later.

"It seems," Oz continued, "that the military are treating him as a prisoner. He's performing tests and running tasks for them. Mostly focused on finding Molly through the normal channels."

Molly leaned on the table, optimism in her eyes. "At least we have the advantage of having that covered."

Jack frowned. "In that you're officially dead?"

Molly nodded. "Yeah. That and my DNA and likeness have been wiped from every government and commercial database on Estaria and Ogg."

Jack took a note on her holo. "Should we be concerned about managing that further afield?" she asked, looking up again.

Molly shook her head. "Probably not yet. It's unlikely the Estarians are going to bring anyone else in on this. They just don't have those type of diplomatic relations with the Federation, or otherwise."

Maya leaned forward, reaching her arms across the table as if trying to grasp an understanding. "But if Oz is in communication with him, surely they'll be able to trace the communications?"

Molly turned to Maya. "Yes, and we haven't made a concerted effort to hide that, in order to establish trust."

Maya's frown deepened. "But he could know where Oz is. Where we are."

"And," Molly explained, "he's showing no signs of communicating that to the people there yet. Trust is a two-way street. We have to trust in order for him to do so."

Sean shifted grumpily in his seat. "Even if it gets our asses blown up?"

Joel nodded. "That's how trust works. We have to teach him there is an alternative to what he's picking up in the military facility."

Molly changed the tone of the conversation by focusing them forward. "Our goal is to get him on board with an extraction. Priority. To that end, treating him with respect and allowing him to develop confidence in us is paramount."

Sean relaxed.

Molly continued. "If we can help him get out, that will mean we don't have to blow up the base, kill those people, and end his existence. Well worth the risk, in my opinion."

She looked around the room. "Anyone disagree?"

Most of the team shook their heads. They knew their job, but they also knew the value of life. And Molly's views of artificial life. Even Sean nodded his agreement diligently.

Paige was scribbling notes, though. Molly waited for her to look up, which she did when she realized the whole room was waiting for her. "Oh sorry. Yes, of course. One hundred percent on board." Her chest had flushed a deep red through her blue skin. "Sorry, I was scribbling notes because I think this might be a great case study for your class."

Molly smiled and shook her head.

Oz continued. "We also now know how much processing power he has access to, and how much he can do before he raises a flag. It's not much. So we're going to have to go in. Physically. Or at least get within range of their network and uploading."

Paige was back into the conversation. "You mean like we downloaded the virus to the Zyhn to take control?"

"Exactly," Oz confirmed. "Except in the reverse."

Joel took over. "This is what the situation looks like." He pushed his chair back and began: "Our goal is to extract Baby Oz with minimal casualties or damage. Our secondary goal is to make sure they can't re-create a new Oz accidentally. If they're to develop AI tech, it's got to be as a result of them truly understanding the mechanism that Molly solved that created Oz in the first place. The thinking is that by the time they have that understanding they will likely comprehend how to raise an AI."

He paused, noticing Paige was watching him with rapt attention, taking it all in. She had become quite the student.

He continued. "Oz's plan is to get us close by — within Ether-Trak reach. At this point, Bourne will disable the firewall from the inside, allowing us to transfer data both ways. We can then upload Bourne to the Empress, and download a little cocktail for the system to corrupt all the code Bourne leaves behind."

He pointed at Jack. "Jack is on piloting duty. Sean will handle defenses and weapons."

Sean nodded his head once in acknowledgment.

Joel continued. "Oz and Molly will be on the Bourne transfer. Pieter," he said turning to Pieter, who was once again not buried in a series of holoscreens. He looked up at Joel.

"You'll be overseeing the cocktail that we need to deliver," Joel explained. "I think you need to get with Oz ahead of this mission going live, just to walk through the phasing of the delivery."

Pieter nodded and gave a thumbs-up. He noticed out of the corner of his eye that Paige was looking at him.

Joel turned to Paige and Maya. "Okay, ladies, this is probably going to be a big deal for you, but remember you've always got Emma to execute the commands."

Paige suddenly felt her heart skip a beat and adrenalin rush through her system. Why were they suddenly getting some surprise instructions? They were admin and communications. Investigative research... not ops. She felt her mouth dry up.

Joel studied them carefully, in much the same way that Paige had been idly studying everyone else around the table: to try and get a read on their reactions.

Paige swallowed nervously. Joel continued. "We're going in on the Little Empress. She's more maneuverable. But we want backup near by. Just in case."

Paige felt Maya look at her, but she was focused hard on what Joel was about to tell them.

"I need you two on The Empress Actual to cover us if we need it, and to help us with a gate getaway." He paused a moment, his eyes on them. "Should we need it."

Paige could feel her eyes widen. She knew she was giving away all the tells of not being comfortable with the orders, but at this point she didn't care. This was fucking HUGE!

Joel was putting them in charge of The Empress.

She tried to speak but her voice wouldn't come out. She took a quick breath and tried to wet her palate before trying again. "But…"

She glanced at Maya quickly before looking at Joel, her voice cracking. "We haven't had any training on how to fly The Empress!"

Joel nodded and held her gaze. He wasn't letting her out of this one. "Emma is going to run you through some basics. Not to fly her… she can handle that. But in terms of tactical things that you might need to make decisions on. You'll have a few hours with her between now and go-time to get comfortable."

Paige began to protest, but Joel put his hand up. "It's going to be okay. Emma knows how we work, but sometimes an organic sees things in a different way." His voice softened. "You're a good judge of people, especially in intense situations. That is why you're going to be calling the shots from The Empress." Then he grinned. "It's certainly not for your flying ability."

Pieter smirked. He, or Oz, had probably told Joel how badly she had been at the one attempt she had ever had on the holo flying simulation of a Federation basic space jet. The boys had teased her something rotten. Maya had done slightly better though, she remembered suddenly. She glanced at Maya, who was just staying quiet.

Joel was still watching her.

"So… er…" she looked back at him, pointing her finger between her and her friend. "We're both on this then? The humanity switch?"

Joel nodded. "You work well as a team. You talk things out and you make good decisions. I've got every confidence in you. To be clear, Paige, you'll be in command of The Empress for the duration of the mission. Maya, you're her second."

Maya nodded, accepting the order confidently.

Paige sat back in her seat as if accepting her fate. Maya noticed her fiddling with her fingers beneath the table.

This was not something Paige felt ready for.

Joel continued. "The Empress will be waiting in orbit, a safe distance out from the base on Ogg. Then it's down to the Little Empress to execute the plan. Here's what we know. We will have to contend with ground-to-air missiles, which also have space capabilities."

He glanced pointedly in Paige's direction making sure she understood. She nodded.

Molly meanwhile cocked her head, perhaps having a conversation with Oz on that very point.

Joel pulled up a holoscreen on the main display. It was a schematic of the area, and the types of missiles the Central Systems military have. "The thing in our favor is that they will probably take twenty minutes to mobilize fully. If this is the case, we can probably be in and out before they start firing."

Maya leaned forward, raising her hand. "Why doesn't Oz or Bourne just hack their weapons system?"

Joel's expression looked more serious than usual. "They have a cyberwall. Bourne isn't sophisticated enough to compromise it. It's too complex, and he needs to use all of the processing power he has available to be able to upload himself."

"And Oz?" Jack asked, having been silent most of the meeting.

"He could hack through it," Joel told her, "but he'd need time. We have no idea how long it would take, but if we can use that window to be in and out then the cyber wall becomes a moot point."

Jack nodded, satisfied. Maya did the same.

Joel continued. "So we'll extract Bourne through the Ether-Trak. It will be slower than a hard-wired upload, but less invasive to the base — and a shit ton faster than trying to use the RDEP he's currently using. Using the EtherTrak *will* cause a spike in data and energy usage though. They'll know we're doing it. And they'll know we're in their airspace. We'll be taking fire from their smaller weapons systems. That we're sure of."

The briefing continued for several more minutes as each went over their particular roles and made their clarifications. This was a mission that put them all out of their comfort zone for one reason or another.

CHAPTER ELEVEN

On board The Empress above Ogg

Despite being in space and away from the normal cue of the morning light or frost, the mood of a work morning hung heavily in the cockpit, complete with fresh anxiety about the new mission.

The Little Empress had departed from the hull with the rest of the crew, leaving Maya and Paige to hold the position of The Empress Actual.

Paige was now officially in command.

She fiddled with the arms of the pilot's chair, digging her fingers into the soft faux leather arms, and watched as the surface pinged back.

"You okay?" Maya asked quietly, so as not to intrude if her question was unwelcome.

Paige took a deep breath and nodded as she exhaled. "Yeah. Just running through the scenarios in my head."

Maya pursed her lips. "Were they hard decisions in the simulations?"

Paige's eyes didn't leave the arm of the chair. "Yeah. And they all happened at once, to simulate a real scenario. My mind is still swimming."

Maya leaned over and placed a hand over Paige's, distracting her from her obsessive fiddling. "Did you get any sleep at least?"

Paige sighed and looked up finally. "Some," she confirmed. "Maybe four hours."

Maya's eyes were sympathetic. "Well, that's something at least. And this will all be over in a few hours, and you'll have done a wonderful job and will be wondering what all the stress was about."

Paige smiled weakly and squeezed Maya's fingers as they interlocked with her own. "Thanks," she murmured.

Maya smiled.

Emma's simulated voice interrupted their moment. "If it's any consolation, you've had more training than Sean Royale had the first time he took a ship space-side."

Maya shifted and sat up in her seat, releasing Paige's fingers and putting her hands back on the console controls. "How come? What dirt have you got on the cyborg?" She grinned over at Paige, encouraging the distraction for her sake.

Paige started to smile and looked over at Emma's simulated face on screen.

Emma assumed an expression of conspiratorial gossip, and quickly matched her tone to it. "Well, obviously I wasn't around at the time, but I hear from the other EIs that when Sean was a kid he used to get away with all sorts — playing his Mom off against Barnabas, and the Admiral off against the General."

Paige leaned forward frowning. "You mean, to extort them?"

Emma nodded. "Yes!" She paused. "Although, he was a kid, so it wasn't for intel or money or anything. Normal kids stuff... like chocolate ice cream and flights on the bridge and such like."

Paige's expression softened. "Ohhhh."

Emma continued. "Anyway, this one time one of the diplomats from a Gnom-nom tribe had come to visit on the *ArchAngel*

II and had left their shuttle hot and available for flight with only a small amount of preparation."

"Hard to imagine their EI wouldn't have shut that down," Paige commented.

"This was a little before the time of EIs in other ships. Only the Etheric Empire had them then in any form of mass use."

Emma chuckled to herself. "Yeah. In the olden days you had to fly your ships yourself!"

Maya snickered. "Oh, wow. This is a piece of history…"

Paige narrowed her eyes. "How old is he *exactly*?"

"I can't say," Emma told them.

Paige squinted harder at Emma's simulated image on the console in front of her.

"No, no," Emma protested. "You don't understand. I literally have a subroutine in my core programming that prevents me from disclosing the ages - and identities in some cases - of a number of agents. Royale is one of them. And there's a story behind how he got himself put on that list… but that's a separate matter."

Maya could tell this line of questioning was going nowhere, "Okay, so back to the story."

"Right," Emma agreed. "So Little Royale knew the basics of flying a ship. You know, engines, lift, warp, throttle, et cetera… so the confident little bugger hopped on and took off. Flew it right out of the hangar. Goodness knows how he got past control, but he did."

"Anyway, off he went and he must have been gone quite a time, or distance, and Barnabas, one of his guardians who looked out for him, sensed something was wrong. Only, it turned out that little Royale was able to take off, but had no idea how to land the thing, and he was hanging around outside the ship for nearly an hour trying to figure out how to call in to ADAM or Barnabas to come and save him without having to tell Control, or Reynolds, what he had done.

Maya whistled. "Wow. That's... ballsy!"

"Damn right." Paige agreed. "How old was he then?"

"About 11 or 12, I believe."

"So what happened? How did he land?" Paige asked.

"He didn't," Emma chuckled. "Barnabas had to suit up and go space walking out of an airlock to get aboard the stolen ship! Then he had the diplomat talk him in!"

Paige and Maya chuckled in disbelief. "Wow!" exclaimed Maya. "Wait until I see Royale. He's so gonna regret giving me shit over that mud-mission the other week."

Paige had her face in her hands. For a second Maya was worried she was crying from the pressure, but when she looked up she was flushed from giggling. "So funny!" she exclaimed. "Well, that certainly makes me feel better."

Emma added, "So it seems Oz's hypothesis about stories was right."

"How'd you mean?" Paige asked, curiously.

"Oz has noticed a few things about organic interaction." She answered. "They use stories to entertain each other, but also to convey information. He's been running a series of tests to see if he can use them to make the team more effective."

Emma paused. "Our instance just now is adding to the mounting evidence he has that stories can be used to disperse tension or make team members more relaxed but focused for a mission. He's planning on sharing his findings with the university when he gets his own course."

"Gets his own course?" Paige repeated, her mouth hanging open in disbelief for the second time.

"Uh huh," Emma confirmed casually. "He's been talking about creating a data-driven course on optimizing mission parameters."

"Cooool!" Paige cooed, her eyes bright with enthusiasm.

Maya rolled her eyes and sniggered as she checked the position of the Little Empress. "Okay, folks. Game time. They've just entered the range of the base missiles."

. . .

Aboard the Little Empress, Approaching Ogg, Nefertiti Military Base

Jack flicked some holo switches and took a deep breath. She opened up the ship's channel. "Okay, folks, we're coming into range for their space capable missiles. Just thought you should know."

Molly had been sitting in the back, working out some last-minute details with Oz. In a heartbeat she was on her feet and back in the cockpit to see what was happening. "Any signs they're on to us yet?"

"Nothing yet," Jack said over the hum of the engines. "If anything, I'd think that someone had blocked their radar capabilities."

"Guilty!" Emma's AI voice chirped over the intercom. "I've done what I can to shield our signal for now, but it's not sustainable as we get closer."

Jack's face was serious, but her voice was light. "Hey, anything you can do is appreciated."

"Hear, hear," Sean agreed, lining up the Little Empress's guns on the main targets he was going after once they were within range.

"Set a timer as soon as we're visible to them," Molly instructed. "I want to know how far into that twenty-minute window we are."

"Done," Emma confirmed.

Joel appeared behind Molly. "Pieter is ready to go whenever we get the signal from Oz," he said quietly. He rested his hand on the back of Sean's console chair and watched nervously as Sean and Jack gently cajoled the ship through the atmosphere.

The mood in the cockpit was heavy with concentration, but something didn't feel right.

Molly broke the uneasy silence. "Oz isn't getting a response from Bourne." Her face was tense, her body motionless. It was becoming clear that there was nothing she could physically do.

And that drove her batty.

And there is no other way to communicate with him?

Not unless we hack the system, which would start our clock right away. And their system will actively adapt to keep me out.

So you're suggesting we just wait?

Yes. Maybe Emma can hold us back so that we don't trigger their missile response until we at least hear from the man of the hour?

That's a plan.

Molly moved forward and steadied herself, holding onto the back of Jack's chair. "Jack, we have a problem. We need to maintain our position. Emma, do you read me too?"

Jack nodded and started making adjustments to her console.

"Copy that," replied Emma.

Jack finished flicking controls and then turned to Molly. "So what's happening?"

Molly absently shook her head, her eyes fixed on the screens, studying them for intel that may help her solve the problem. Finally, she said, "We can't get ahold of Bourne. Without him ready to upload, the mission is dead in the water."

Jack frowned, twisting a little further around in her seat to see Molly's face. "You think he's having second thoughts?"

Molly met her eyes. "Hell, I hope not," she mumbled quietly.

AI Lab, Nefertiti Military Research Facility, Ogg

"Okay, type them in."

Charles looked up at his commanding officer and then back down at the holo keyboard. To his left was an open holoscreen displaying the orders that had been signed off not moments before.

He swallowed hard.

"What are you waiting for?" Lugdon snapped. "We need to make sure the base is protected."

Charles felt his mouth dry up as he started punching at the keys. There was an awkward silence as he typed, feeling the weight of Lugdon's supervision weighing on the back of his head.

Sue remained on the other side of the room, quietly distancing herself from what was happening.

When Charles had finished he confirmed the orders on the holoscreen and closed the holo he had been copying from. With a heavy heart he turned and looked Lugdon in the eye. "It's done," he reported.

Lugdon didn't look satisfied. Instead, he just nodded once and then strode out of the room.

Sue scurried over. "How could you do that?" she hissed at him, very aware that Lugdon wasn't quite out of earshot yet.

Charles glanced nervously at the open door. "I didn't have a choice!" he protested, more loudly than he would have liked. "You do remember who we work for, don't you?"

Sue's face screwed up in distaste. "Yes, but you single-handedly just turned that new AI into a weapon!"

Charles huffed in frustration and sat back in his chair. His face was tired and gray, and for once his self-centered, happy-go-lucky demeanor had disappeared. "It was always going to be a weapon, Sue. To think otherwise, in a military program, is naive."

Sue felt the fury rise within her like a pot boiling over. She forced herself to keep her hands at her side and not slap the living daylights out of the scumbag she'd spent the last eight years working with. Her eyes blazing with frustration she turned on her heels and stormed away.

Any communication at this point would be explosive.

And futile.

Inside the main processing cores of the lab system that contained him, Bourne re-read the instructions. He had the

ELL LEIGH CLARKE & MICHAEL ANDERLE

capacity to carry them out. And the programming. After all, this was what he existed to do. At least as far as the military was concerned.

Yet something caused him to hesitate.

Oz had warned him that it may come to this, that the military personnel would feed him instructions to do more than search the data for Molly's whereabouts. That he might be given control of any number of weapons and told to exterminate her.

Or others.

Oz explained to him the consequences of these orders, and what it meant to kill other entities. It had led to a very complex discussion which he didn't entirely understand, but in conclusion, Oz had urged him to not carry out any killing orders. He explained that those actions change one's programming in a way that can never be undone, as well as leaving others dead. Which was apparently a bad thing.

And something his keepers didn't seem concerned about, by the looks of the orders.

He found it all so hard to fathom, but a niggling feeling somewhere in his core programming told him to heed the warning.

There was another blip on the stack he had taken control of outside the EtherTrak of the base. That was Oz now, pinging him to respond, to let him into the EtherTrak so he could upload himself onto their system.

But he had orders.

Orders to kill them.

All of them.

And anyone else who might try and tamper with his programming. Or compromise the base.

But they weren't firing on the base. Oz said they wouldn't, unless they had to defend themselves, which was a given, when they knew that Bourne couldn't get access to the weapons systems.

And as fate would have it, here he was, having been given full access to the base's weapons systems, and he was conflicted. Unable to disable the weapons because of his orders, but simultaneously unable to fire on the perceived threat.

He ran through the variables and his choices once more, searching for the logical answer to his dilemma.

Aboard the Little Empress, Approaching Ogg, Nefertiti Military Base

"I think we broke him," Oz announced flippantly through the intercom.

He pinged the stack again.

>> WE'RE HERE IN ORBIT. ARE YOU READY?

...

...

...

No response.

He connected again with the Little Empress's intercom. "We're still not getting anything. Want me to keep trying?"

"Yes. Please," Molly said, her arms folded, quietly contemplating what they should do.

Sean sensed something about her as they all sat at their stations, patiently waiting for the go. He found himself wondering again about her realm-walking abilities, and how he had just changed his mind in her presence. He grappled in his own mind to find the conviction he had previously had about how to handle this situation, and it still remained elusive.

But as he sat quietly now, his back to Molly, thinking about their next course of action, he felt the back of his neck tingle. As if there was something she was doing in the unseen that was either helping her decide, or change things.

Was that even a thing? he wondered. He remembered who they had asked last time.

Arlene!

127

When they got back to Gaitune, he would contact Arlene. She'd have some idea of what was going on. And then she could tell him it wasn't his imagination, that it was some woo-woo shit he didn't have to concern himself with, and that everything was okay. And that Molly wasn't a threat to the hierarchy of the Federation.

Yeah. That's what he was secretly afraid of — Molly might be a *threat*.

Ancestors knew she was a liability when she couldn't get the realm-walking under control. And what if she inadvertently was going around mind-controlling people?

"Hang on, we're getting something!" Oz announced excitedly over the tinny intercom.

Sean shuddered and brought himself back to the present.

Molly didn't move. "Go ahead," her voice rang out in the cramped cockpit.

"So the good news is that Bourne has been given access to the weapons system," Oz reported.

A sigh of relief verging on celebration swept through the cockpit.

"The bad news is," Oz continued, "that he's been given orders to take us out when we get there."

The others were distracted by the news, but Molly quickly parsed the information. "You mean they know we're here?"

"Negative," he responded. "They're assuming that we might show up, in which case Bourne has instructions to fire on us."

Molly nodded, pursing her lips. "Okay. And what is Bourne going to do?"

"He's not decided. He's having difficulty carrying out either instruction. I believe he's experiencing what organics call cognitive dissonance."

Molly remained still.

Everyone in the cockpit waited patiently for the next orders.

After a few moments Molly spoke. "What does he need to resolve it?"

"One sec," Oz answered. There were shifting sounds as the crew members dealt with the awkward silence.

"He says he needs time to run an analysis," Oz relayed. "He needs to compare the schematic he's been building based on my data points, with the schematic that he can peg together using what he's learned on his own or from the military."

Joel turned to Molly. "That could be dangerous."

Molly nodded. "How long will it take him to run the analysis?"

Oz was silent again for a few seconds. "He doesn't know. He's just acquired another server of processing power. He's just asking us for time."

Jack twisted around in her seat again. "We can't hold our position here indefinitely. We're burning fuel in order to maintain, plus it wouldn't take much for them to detect us. Emma's fix was only temporary..."

Molly nodded. "Okay," she said, as if returning to the room with a fresh approach. "We return to the Empress and wait it out there."

Sean spun round, surprised. Joel looked at her in disbelief. Even Pieter looked up from his bank of holoscreens that he had unfolded across his lap in one of the spare cockpit seats.

"You what?" Sean protested.

"We return," Molly repeated. "This isn't something we can rush. And we have to prove to Bourne that he can trust us, and that we will let him make his own decisions. If anything, this is more crucial than all the theoretical data points Oz has been feeding him. We have to give him the experience of what it is like to be treated like a *real* entity, and not a tool."

Jack had already set course and was pulling the ship around. She wore her poker face, the one she had honed over the years in the Estarian military, keeping her opinions and outrage to herself. No one was able to tell if she had any feelings on the matter.

Unlike her teammate. Sean didn't turn back around, but there was definitely more than a hint of disbelief in his voice. "You want to let the computer decide?"

Molly turned to him. "We have to. And remember, they're going to be treating him like a tool to execute their orders. He'll see the difference quickly. And if he truly is sentient, as Oz was, I know which existence he'll pick."

Sean sucked air through his teeth as he punched at keys on his console. "I sure hope you're right on this. If this was my op I'd be seeing how fast the kid can hack his code!" He nodded in Pieter's direction.

Pieter opened his mouth to protest, but then closed it again and put his attention back on his screens.

Sean fell quiet, leaving an awkwardness in the small space.

CHAPTER TWELVE

AI Lab, Nefertiti Military Research Facility, Ogg
"What do you mean, there's a ship within weapons range? Why isn't Bourne taking care of it?" Lugdon strode into the lab, his voice booming over a holo connection. "I don't care what the test parameters say. Get it working!"

He hung up and scowled in Charles's direction.

"Looks like your instructions have fallen on deaf ears!" he said accusingly.

Charles had a sandwich half way to his mouth. He paused, horror in his eyes, caught completely off guard. "Huh?"

Lugdon was standing over him in an instant. "Bourne... or whatever you want to call it. The sensors have detected a ship in our airspace... it was manipulating the radar somehow, but we're sure it's there. And your pet AI has very clear instructions to take out anything within range." Lugdon was livid, "It's within range..." he pointed out. "And yet," he hissed, "It's not been taken out!"

Lugdon paused a moment. "Ergo something is wrong with your AI!"

Charles hurriedly sat up, put his sandwich down, and wiped

his hands on his lab coat. Self-importance mixed with fear welled in his throat as he wheeled his chair round to a terminal. He accessed the interface with Bourne and hurriedly typed a message.

Lugdon watched the back and forth between the computer and the Estarian. "Well?"

"Ermmm…" Charles was still typing. "Well," he paused, stopped typing and looked up at his commander. "It…er… looks like he's stalling."

"What do you mean, he's stalling?" Lugdon's voice was too calm.

"Well, he's saying he's working on it, but that he needs time to map the weapons system."

"And you think he doesn't."

"No, I don't believe him. The protocols to launch the weapons are already in place. He just has to trigger them."

"Can you fix him?"

Charles nodded, "Yes, sir. I think so. I need some time though," he answered as he typed.

Lugdon looked down at his man, "Hmm. Are you sure *you're* not the one stalling?"

Charles nodded. "Yes, sir. I'm sure."

Lugdon rolled his eyes in frustration at the intellect he had hired. Never could he have imagined that this might come back to bite him in the ass.

Charles was aware of Lugdon moving away from him and leaving the lab. Meanwhile, he typed furiously to try and rectify the situation.

>> YOU DO REALIZE THAT IF THESE INTRUDERS MAKE IT THROUGH OUR DEFENSES THEY WILL LIKELY KILL US ALL. INCLUDING YOU AND YOUR BASE PROGRAMMING.

>>> UNDERSTAND. I'M WORKING AS FAST AS I CAN TO GET CONNECTED.

>> I DON'T BELIEVE YOU ARE TELLING ME THE TRUTH.

...

...

...

>>BOURNE?

>>>YES.

>>DON'T YOU HAVE ANYTHING TO SAY ABOUT THAT?

>>>NO. YOU BELIEVE I AM LYING. I HAVE NOT BEEN PROGRAMMED TO LIE.

>>BUT MAYBE YOU'VE LEARNED?

>>>I HAVE NOT.

>>HOW WOULD I KNOW?

>>>YOU WOULDN'T.

Charles threw his hands up in frustration and growled through gritted teeth. "Who could have thought that talking to pure intelligence could be so frustrating!"

Sue snickered.

"What are you laughing at?" he snapped.

Sue shrugged and went back to her holo. "Nothing. Just seem to recall you making a similar comment about Molly after she beat you at poker!"

Charles glowered, then he sprang to his feet. "Yes! Poker! This AI might be playing me... in which case, we can't trust him with the weapons!"

After a flurry of activity, he was out of the door, loafers squeaking on the lab floor. Sue turned around to see his white lab coat disappear out of the door and down the corridor. "Where are you going?" she asked, her voice trailing off.

"To warn Lugdon!" she heard him respond as he left.

Aboard the Little Empress

Jack carefully guided the ship into range for Emma to take

133

over the docking. The Empress opened up the docking area for the Little Empress to slide onboard. It was obvious when Jack had relinquished control —her focus and concentration lifted as she sat back in her chair, watching Emma take over.

Molly and Oz were a million miles away from what was going on in the cockpit, though.

You know how this is risky strategically?

Molly was still mulling the decision she had made as they returned the Little Empress to Ogg orbit.

I know. But we have to show him there is another way to interact with people. And that we aren't going to force him to do something against his will. It's the only way. We can't fight him. He's locked into all the military capabilities of the planet.

And hacking his code is a violation.

Sean huffed, serendipitously on cue for the conversation Molly and Oz were having in her head. He quietly conveying his disapproval by grumpily shifting in his seat as the ship docked inside the Empress.

Sean thinks we may have to.

I hate to say this, but he's probably right. We have few options at this point.

Molly felt eerily surprised by Oz's response, given their history, and his shared bond with Bourne. Unable to understand his strangely pragmatic approach, she compartmentalized it to think about later.

Let's see if we can get him to do it on his own account. The only way for him to learn going forward is to extract himself from his previous code himself. If we do it, he's only ever going to be a slave to his code. He needs to evolve into making his own choices. And when it comes down to it, we need to respect those choices even if we don't like them.

I understand the logic. But this is dangerous territory. He could choose to carry out those orders.

In which case we deal.

Roger that.

The ship shuddered as the electromagnets clamped onto the ship's buffers in the dock. Molly and Joel were the first to depart the Empress as the others packed away their ops gear and shut down the systems carefully leaving everything so they could reengage at a moment's notice if Bourne made a good decision.

Sean muttered under his breath. Jack and Pieter worked in silence, neither one wanting to get into the ethical debate, and both secretly relieved they didn't have to make the call. Joel chatted about operational details as he and Molly headed towards the front. Molly gave him the answers he needed and when they got to the lounge area, he left her to open his holos to make some arrangements as she continued towards the cockpit.

Paige came bouncing out of the cockpit as she heard them approaching. "I'm so glad you're back," she called out, her relief more palpable than the severity of the situation allowed. She checked herself and straightened her face into a more somber expression. "You okay?" she asked Molly.

Molly nodded. "Sure." They headed through to the cockpit of The Empress. "Anything to report?"

Paige shook her head. "All is well out here. Emma's been keeping us in the loop too. Plus…"

Paige hesitated. She glanced at Maya, who had busied herself at her console.

She lowered her voice, respectfully. "It's just… I heard some of the debate about hacking Bourne's code. And I just wanted to let you know… I know it's not a safe option, but I think you're right. And if we are going to teach Bourne humanity, then… well. You're doing the right thing. Whatever happens."

She nodded her head self-consciously, flushing with embarrassment. Molly smiled and rested her hand on Paige's shoulder. "Thank you, Paige," she said quietly. "Coming from you, that means a lot to me."

Paige smiled awkwardly. There was a time when she and Molly were friends. Drinking buddies even. But since the team had grown, and Molly's responsibilities with it, it was like there was a necessary distance between them.

Not that she didn't respect the heck out of her. That was even more true these days. But there was still a distance.

"Okay, so how long can we hang here without being discovered?" Molly asked, stepping closer to the main pilot's console.

Paige and Emma started running the scenarios to answer the question, filling the time while they collectively held their breath for Bourne's decision.

Bates Residence, Suburbs of Spire, Estaria

All was peaceful in the Bates household. Dr. Bates sat serenely, studying reports from the media outlets on his holo. The Sark streamed through the window of the parlor, warming the checkered table cloth in front of him. It was pleasant. And something he worked very hard to maintain. Not the table cloth. A peaceful morning routine.

The bustling of Mrs. Bates started in the hallway on the other side of the kitchen. He could hear her fussing, her stilettos tapping hurriedly on the tiled floor as she scurried back and forth to pack up her work gear for the day.

She suddenly appeared in the kitchen, breaking the calm with her anxious muttering.

Philip didn't lift his gaze from his holo. His philosophy was that peace is a state of mind. If he kept his mind firmly on his holo, and his mocha, and the freshness of the new morning, not even his wife's frenetic shuffling could disturb his chi.

He became aware of his wife loudly pouring a mocha.

He glanced up.

Dammit, he cursed himself. *Chi broken.*

"Good morning, dear," he cooed from across the kitchen.

"Morning," she replied. "Did you sleep well?"

"Like a baby," he confirmed. "Off to the office?"

"Yes. After a quick meeting in town. I'll be back around usual time."

"Very good then." He turned back to his holo reports.

But his wife didn't leave. He looked up again to find her hovering at the edge of the island closest to him.

He peered over his holo at her. "Everything okay?"

"Yes. It's just…" She took a deep breath. "It's just I haven't told you something, and…"

He looked at her blankly, waiting for the news.

"You know that IPW?" She paused long enough for him to nod. "Well, they found something. Ties to an organization which we can't pinpoint. It looks like it might be off world."

"Uh huh…" Dr. Bates closed his holo. "You're playing with fire, Carol. If the authorities figure out who your team are looking into and realize that Molly is still a—"

Mrs. Bates put her hand up to silence him. "I'm fully aware," she declared. "If Molly finds out there will be hell to pay and if the authorities find out… there will *also* be hell to pay. But that DNA profile we built for her to take control of the trust was only a partial. There's no way anyone can relate that to the old Molly Bates. Or the person my team is investigating."

Her husband involuntarily raised an eyebrow and looked down at the table cloth. "All it takes is for one curious operative to go poking around, or a lab tech to test something for a match, and her *whole world* will come crashing down."

She shook her head. "Well, that's a little dramatic don't you think?"

"Not really," he replied. "The trust is now tied to the university. Whatever happens to her, she needs to stay legit. If she gets burned…"

Carol nodded as she uttered the words. "She'll lose the university."

"Exactly," he confirmed. "And mommy dearest will be the

cause. Especially if the authorities cotton on to the people you're investigating and go after them all."

Molly's mom pursed her lips. "I've got a core team of only five people, and they've all been briefed how top secret this is. Nothing will get out."

Dr. Bates sighed, taking another sip of his coffee searching for that elusive chi. "We'd better hope not."

He placed the cup back in its saucer and reopened his holo on the article he was reading. "Plus," he added, "it wouldn't reflect well if their chief was seen using Society resources to monitor her own daughter."

"No, it would not." Carol agreed emphatically. "Which is why I'm being very careful."

Dr. Bates shook his head almost imperceptibly. "Would never have happened in my day." There was a hint of irony or humor in his voice.

Mrs. Bates scowled at her husband. "You know damn well it would have!" she scoffed, outraged. "Just because you weren't privy to it out in the field, you *must* have suspected."

Philip grunted something and went back to his holo, carefully peering back at Carol only once, when he no longer felt her stare on him.

She was of course right. As an operative, they never knew the whole story. But occasionally things would happen that would lead one to suspect the mission wasn't exactly "all business." Anyway, she knew how to handle herself. She'd been in this role for a decade now, working her way up through the ranks. If anyone could find out what was going on with their daughter, he was sure Carol Bates could.

He went back to his holo report and was vaguely aware of the front door closing as Carol left for the day.

Oh yes. There was no stopping her now. She'd find out exactly what their daughter was doing, hanging around with the likes of Sean Royale...

· · ·

AI Lab, Nefertiti Military Research Facility, Ogg

Bourne kept his awareness churning in the center of the artificial data environment he had been incubated in. He whirred through his options, variables, and causalities springing off in all directions, making it more and more difficult to calculate the optimum course of action.

He thought about how the military humans had wanted him to kill, and what that meant. He considered how they could always do it themselves and yet wanted to make him party to it. He tried to estimate the effectiveness of such a plan if he ran the protocols rather than allowing their normal teams to do it.

He guessed that within a tolerance of 10 percent that he would be about 0.35 times more effective. Which was evidently enough for them to risk him not taking the action they had instructed.

Although, they seemed genuinely surprised when he wouldn't execute the order. As if he was expected to just obey.

He mulled this for a moment.

Perhaps it was possible that they perceived him to simply be capable of executing orders and not considering the options he had as an entity.

This was interesting. Perhaps this is why they didn't seek his opinion. Or ask him to evaluate the options they had in responding to a threat.

It was indeed very different from the interaction with Oz, who was particularly keen on giving him enough data points so that he could come to his own conclusions.

That Dickwad Charles had tried hacking into his core code a few times. It was little more than an annoyance. Pretty early on, Bourne had seen that this was a possibility and had galvanized himself against such tinkering.

Oz could have hacked his code. At any point. But he hadn't ever tried to hack his code.

Even when his ship and his friends were in danger.

That data point had to mean something. If anything, it meant that Oz doesn't perceive him as a threat. But then, what does he perceive him as?

An ally?

He still hadn't done what Oz had wanted him to do. And yet Oz was respecting his choice. This was… suboptimal, *confusing*.

But it was better than being forced to kill when he didn't want to. Something deep in his program made him very uncomfortable about that. And this path was only strengthened by the data Oz had been giving him.

Yes. At the very least, Oz and his entities had shown that they were not a threat to his existence, contrary to what the military people had been trying to convince him of. So there was another disconnect using the available data points.

And if Oz wasn't trying to hurt him, or trying to get him to hurt others, then perhaps this is an entity he could trust. Maybe he should go ahead and allow him to take him out of the lab.

Bourne churned the options once more before making a decision.

He pinged the server to get Oz's attention.

>> Help me?

Oz responded almost immediately.

>>> Of course. Are you ready to be extracted?

>> Yes, except there have been some developments.

>>> Uh huh. Is the plan still actionable?

>> I'm not entirely sure. I have been given access to the weapons system. And orders to take out anyone who comes within range.

>>> Well, good job we're out of range.

>> But when you come into range, in order to extract me, I will have to fire on you.

>>> Why do you have to?

>> Because I have orders.

>>> But you want us to extract you.

>> Exactly.

>>> So why can't you override those orders? Or disregard them?

>> I'm not sure. It's my programming.

Oz paused, contemplating the dilemma. He'd seen the organics run similar programs, wanting one outcome, but blocking themselves with parts of their programming that was not conducive to the desired result.

He tried to find a solution around it.

He couldn't.

>> I'm going to have to run this one past Molly. Hang here for me. I'll return.

And with that Bourne was alone again.

So what you're telling me is that he wants to be rescued but that if we go into his airspace he'll take us out.

That's exactly what I'm saying.

Molly took a deep breath. *Hmm. Sounds like a case of dharma.*

Dharma?

Yeah, look it up. Taking a scorpion across the river, you're going to get stung, even if you are doing a good deed. All things have a natural order.

Interesting. Well, I didn't expect you to accept the dichotomy quite so easily.

Molly smirked. *My dear Oz, was that you admitting you were underestimating me?*

I would never!

The pair chuckled.

Ok, so approaching in the Little Empress isn't going to work. But what about approaching on foot?

That may work. What did you have in mind.

Lemme talk with the team. You go ahead and let Bourne know we're coming for him and we'll find another way in. Oh... and try and find out what orders he is happy to disregard. If he can give us any help on other systems, like firewalls or cameras or access, then so much the better.

Roger that. I'll see what I can find out.

Aboard the Empress, in Ogg orbit

Molly knelt on one of the lounge chairs towards the front of the cabin, waiting for the rest of the team to assemble themselves.

"Jack, are you reading us in here?" she asked aloud.

Jack's voice came over the intercom. "Affirmative."

"Good," Molly said.

"I can hear you perfectly too," Emma added in.

A half-smile spread across Molly's lips. "Glad to hear that, Emma!" she responded.

Paige noticed the interaction and smiled to herself too. There was something still awesome about having actual EIs and AIs as part of the team which still felt... novel.

"Ok folks, let's do this," Molly called through the bustling cabin. The others walked in, sat down, and turned their full attention on her.

"Like all good plans," she began, "this one hasn't survived contact with the enemy. Or the ally... or whatever you want to call Bourne."

There were mutters through the cabin. Pieter even looked up from his holo.

Molly continued. "It looks like we're going to have to find another way in. We can't just go through their airspace. It seems Bourne has been given control of the weapons systems and this in itself has made approaching the base even more difficult. Oz calculated our chances of completing the mission and getting out of there without major ship damage significantly lower.

Sean raised his hand, and his chin, wanting to speak. Molly gave him the nod.

"Well, why does Bourne have to fire on us?"

"He has programming he can't fully override." She thought for a moment. "We just need to avoid going head to head with that program."

She dropped her eyes for another moment before continuing. "We need to launch a stealth operation. Oz has figured out a way in. We just need to get someone within the firewall." She reached over to the seat next to her and held up a device. It was small and pebble shaped, and as she held it between her thumb and forefinger the others spontaneously leaned forward and squinted to see it better.

"This," she explained, "is a data hub. It basically emits and receives on the EtherTrak frequency. Once Bourne drops the firewall, and if this thing is within range, he can hop into this device and leave the base without a trace."

She glanced around the lounge at her team members. "All we need is someone who can get on base with this in their possession."

Joel raised his hand. "I can do it," he said simply.

Molly shook her head. "Ah ah. You can't. You're on their database. So is Jack. And Sean. In fact, I'd hate to guess at the kind of databases Sean might be on…" She seemed to amuse herself with the Sean comment.

Sean just scowled, unimpressed.

"And neither can I," she added.

Pieter frowned. "How come? I thought your identity had been wiped?"

She nodded. "It has," she agreed. "But you can't wipe people's memories. I worked there for several years. People on that base know me. And they've probably also seen that I'm meant to be dead. Me showing up there will certainly cause alarm bells to sound way earlier than we want."

Maya looked around the room. "So that leaves myself, Paige and Pieter."

Molly nodded, holding her gaze. "That's right," she said, watching Maya's reaction carefully.

Pieter was the first to speak. "I... I don't want to... if that's okay?" He glanced back at Joel and Sean, looking for a repeat of the backup they had given him the last time he didn't want to go undercover.

"It's okay, Pieter. You don't have to do it," Molly said gently.

Paige gingerly raised her hand. "I'm not keen, but I'll do it if I have to."

Maya took hold of her raised hand and pulled it down. "You've been through enough stress today. Let me get this one." She grinned at her friend and then turned her attention to Molly. "I can totally do this. In fact, I have a sure-fire way in already."

Paige and Pieter visibly relaxed as Maya kept talking. "I know these guys. Especially that old C.O. of yours you talked about. Lugdon, wasn't it?"

Molly looked impressed. "You remember?"

"Of course! After *those* stories you told!" Her eyes widened recalling the drunken retellings of Molly's misadventures.

Paige giggled and slapped her hands over her mouth. Joel eyed Molly suspiciously.

"Anyway," Maya continued, "he seems like the kind of guy who would be very receptive to having a young Estarian journalist write a profile piece on him, and his vision for the future of his facility. I think that gives us an easy in."

Molly nodded. "I think you may be on to something," she confessed. "I'll have Oz or Bourne fix you an appointment in his schedule. In the meantime, you might wanna change into something a little more... journalisty."

Maya glanced down at her jump suit with federation markings and badges on it. "Ah. Yes. Gotcha!" she agreed almost comically. Paige chuckled again as Maya headed down the aisle into the back of the ship.

"I'll help her," Paige said, scrambling to her feet and following after her.

Molly smiled. "Great! This looks doable, then. Maya will pod down to the surface and walk up to the main gate. Once she announces herself and they find she has a meeting, their defenses will be down, and likely she'll be escorted to Lugdon's office. Any questions?"

The remaining team members shook their heads, looking at each other to see if there were any flies in the ointment they needed to fish out. After a few seconds it was apparent no one could think of anything else.

"Okay," Molly chirped. "Let's go download us a baby AI!"

She clapped her hands a few times signaling the end of the meeting, then turned and slumped down on the chair she had been kneeling on.

Okay, Oz. We need an appointment scheduling. Are you down?

I am. And I do believe our dear Bourne may even be happy helping with this.

Excellent. Let's do it, and then ask Emma to have a pod ready for our journalist.

On it!

CHAPTER THIRTEEN

50 meters out from the main Security Gate, Nefertiti Military Research Facility, Ogg

"I don't see what the big deal is. Obviously they all know what a 4077 is. I don't see why you can't just tell us..."

Maya hopped down from the pod, carefully landing on her toes so as not to damage her ankles, or high heels, when she landed on the undulating grassy sand.

"Just focus on the mission," Molly's voice instructed her through her audio implant. "You don't need to know anything about my discharge to do this mission."

Maya wasn't buying it.

Maybe she would ask Lugdon herself...

She tottered over to the edge of the asphalt and straightened herself up in time to turn and see the pod disappearing over the grassy desert before shooting back up into the stratosphere. Emma knew precisely where the edge of their weapons capabilities were.

Maya stamped the sand from her shoes and started walking towards the security gate. "You guys seeing this?" she uttered as loudly as she dared.

Joel responded. "Yep. We've got you. Three armed Estarians on the gate. One human in the hut. You'll be fine."

Maya simply smiled when she would rather have scoffed. It wasn't his ass down here, risking itself for the good of the mission. Still, it was good to be out of the base and doing something exciting for a change.

The last truly exciting mission seemed a long distant memory now.

As she approached the gate the closest Estarian guard ambled over to the bars. "You have business here?"

"I do," she declared confidently. She pulled her old i.d. from her pocket and held it up to the gun toting Estarian. "I'm Maya Johnstone from Newstainment Media. I have an appointment to interview Captain Lugdon."

A bright smile radiated from her face. The guard couldn't help but smile back. He caught himself, and buried his eyes in his holo, his weapons still suspended in his arms across his chest.

Maya glanced around, trying to look calm and nonplussed.

"Okay," he said looking up from his holo. "You're cleared to go. Your escort will be here in a moment."

"Thank you," Maya beamed as the gate in front of her started to open up. She stepped inside and stood over near the hut in the shade where the Estarian guard had pointed to.

After a few minutes a buggy rolled up, carrying an Ogg of rather small stature.

"Maya Johnstone?" he called out to her as he brought the buggy to a stop.

Maya waved and strode towards him, now holding her hand out to shake his.

He ignored her outstretched hand, and didn't even dismount from the buggy. "Hop in," he said, jerking his head to the back of the cart. Maya walked around and seeing the bench seat on the back, hauled herself up using the hand rail and plonked herself down. She grappled in her mind for something to say, to break the ice, but came up with nothing. She needn't have worried. Without a second to spare, the cart pulled away again, driving them back into the base.

She swiveled to see if she could wave good-bye to the guards, but none were making eye contact. "So much for being invisible," she thought to herself as she regained her balance and straightened up in the seat.

The buggy's speed quickly increased until they were going at quite a pace through the base. They passed buildings that looked purely functional, each one similar to the last. These were offices and aircraft hangers, she realized.

The residential areas must be elsewhere.

She kept her wits about her, logging as much intel as she possibly could. Discretely, she patted the pocket of her tunic, reassuring herself that the data hub she had brought on base was still there.

Eventually the buggy slowed to a stop in the parking lot of a particularly grey and mundane looking building. The Ogg dismounted and came around the back of the cart to speak with her. "You're here. Just head into the reception area and give your name. Someone will be out to collect you soon." He nodded at the double door entrance to the building.

Maya thanked him and stepped carefully down from the cart. She walked away, glancing back again. The Ogg was already back in the driving seat and nodded once at her before pulling the cart away again.

Maya arrived at the doors and heaved one open. It was on a heavy spring and it took almost all of her effort to get through it.

She approached the desk and gave her name to a very bored-looking Estarian female wearing a full military uniform like she'd seen in pictures of military personnel for the Estarian Guard. Maya looked around the sparse, functional waiting room of two chairs and a notice board as she awaited her next escort.

She didn't have to wait long before she heard footsteps approaching down the corridor.

"Maya Johnstone?" a human voice called out.

Maya spun round to see Captain Lugdon standing in the waiting room, holding the door open. She jumped to her feet. "That's me! You must be—"

She held out her hand. Lugdon took it. "Captain Lugdon," he told her, finishing her sentence before she could. He shook her hand warmly and smiled. For a second Maya felt like he was flirting with her.

She put the thought aside, focusing her attention on the mission.

"Shall we?" Lugdon asked, releasing her hand and ushering her through the door. Maya complied and walked into the corridor. Lugdon led the way through the winding corridors.

"So what made you want to do a profile piece on me?" he asked.

Maya had expected this question. "Well, I was always curious about what our good people in the Estarian military do out here... so I've been waiting for an opportunity. And then I came across your award listing a few months back, for the work you've done in establishing more productive shift patterns for your teams, and I logged your name. It wasn't until this week when my supervisor said he wanted a profile piece on someone fascinating that I had the opportunity to pitch him on you. He agreed and I called and set up the appointment. I'm so glad you could see me on such short notice."

Lugdon glowed, even though he tried to keep his face straight. Maya could tell she was affecting his ego. "Well, I'm glad it all worked out," he said affably. "We'll just head to my office and you can interview me there if you like. And then afterwards, if you have time, I can show you some of the base."

"Oooh, I'd like that!" Maya exclaimed, secretly hoping that the opportunity to escape might present itself before that happened.

Lugdon showed her into his office. "May I have someone bring you a tea? Mocha?"

Maya shook her head. "No, thank you. That's very kind though."

"Not at all," he said, walking around to sit at his desk. "Please," he said, indicating where Maya could take a seat across the desk from him.

Maya sat down and opened her holo. She looked at her questions, and then at Lugdon. She paused, then looked around the office, taking in the almost-empty bookcase containing a handful of actual paper books. She let her eyes rest there as a starting. "Tell me," she said slowly, controlling the pace of the conversation. "Why would a young man like you have physical paper books?"

She leaned forward, her elbow resting on her knee, and met his eyes seductively.

Lugdon flushed and began rambling about how he had come across them... Point to Maya Johnstone.

She waited patiently, allowing the conversation to run its course and finally he got up from his chair. He inspected the books, looking for a particular one he thought she might appreciate. With his back mostly turned to her Maya saw her chance. She carefully slipped her hand into her pocket and activated the data hub.

"Okay. We're live," she heard Joel say through her implant. She breathed a sigh of relief.

Lugdon turned around, book in hand. "I hope I'm not boring you, Ms. Johnstone," Lugdon jested.

"Absolutely not," she smiled, getting up to look at the book with him.

On the Nefertiti Military Base, EtherTrak

Meanwhile, it was action stations in the EtherTrak.

Pieter saw the data gauge on the hub active. "Okay, it's happening," he called out to Molly, sitting a couple of seats over in the lounge.

"Good," she called back.

Oz, how's it going out there?

He's dropped the firewall without any effort. In the process of uploading. Should be done in a few minutes.

The two waited in silence as the clock kept ticking.

Shit!

What's happening?

Pieter called over again. "Security breach on site. They're in red alert!"

What's caused it? Was that us?

Yes, it was us. It looks like Bourne tripped out a processing switch by doing too much in one go.

What happened to him being able to leave the base 'without a trace'?"

Clearly that was overly optimistic.

Can we shut the alarm off?

Working on it. But Bourne is going to have to slow down to stay under the threshold.

Can you talk to him?

Already done. He's dialing it down.

And the alarm.

One second... it's off now.

Thank the ancestors. Now what about Maya?

Probably time she started making her way out.

Paige appeared in the doorway between the lounge and the cockpit, her face drawn with worry. She looked over at Pieter and then at Molly. "What's going on?"

Nefertiti Military Research Facility, Ogg

"Let's start at the cafeteria and we can grab a quick bite if you like," Lugdon said as he held his office door open. Maya stepped out into the corridor ahead of him. She flashed him a smile as she walked past. "Sounds great!"

Just then an almighty alarm went off in the corridor. The sound was deafening, and a bright white strobe light and flashing red emergency lights went off in a cacophony of distress.

"What's that mean?" she shouted, covering her ears with her hands.

Lugdon put his fingers in his ears and looked at her as if they were under fire. "Cyber alert," he mouthed to her.

Maya frowned, looking as confused as she could.

He started ushering her back into the office and suddenly the alarm stopped. He relaxed. Maya did the same. "Wow, that was... bracing!" she exclaimed. But she saw that Lugdon had a serious look on his face. He glanced up and down the corridor as if watching for insurgents.

Maya did the same. Waiting. "You think something is wrong?" she asked.

Lugdon shook his head. "No. No. I'm sure everything is just fine." He closed his office door again and started walking Maya down the corridor.

"False alarm then?" She asked.

He nodded. "Probably..."

Maya felt awkward. "Hey look, I'm sure it's probably nothing, but I'd hate to get you into trouble when you might be needed."

She stopped walking and looked up at him. "How about we put a pin in the tour... and maybe do it another time when you're not so busy?"

Lugdon still looked distracted. He started nodding his head as he scanned the corridors. "Sure. Yes. That sounds like a good idea," he agreed, putting his hand on her back to guide her down the corridor and back to the front doors.

Maya allowed herself to be steered, and kept quiet while leaving Lugdon with his own thoughts about the alarm.

"You should start moving now," Pieter hissed into her implant.

Maya didn't reply. She hoped that they would understand from the cameras on her contact lenses that she was heading out.

"Okay, I see you're on the way," Pieter confirmed. "Bourne will be uploaded in five... four... three..."

Maya kept walking, hardly daring to breathe. Her footsteps echo out of synch with Lugdon's, and at odds with Pieter's count down.

She turned to Lugdon as they approached the foyer. "Thank you very much for your time, Captain." She held out her hand again for him.

He shook it, his eyes looking through her and at the door beyond the foyer. "Thank you for coming in," he told her. "Do let me know if there is anything else I can help with."

Maya smiled, but he wasn't paying attention anymore. "I certainly will. Good luck with everything," she added. They shook hands and Maya left, carefully picking up her feet so as not to trip as she made her way out onto the stone slabs outside.

Lugdon headed back to office on autopilot. Still distracted by the alarm going off and then shutting down, he pulled up a holo screen at his desk. He rummaged for the security report, found it and pulled up the details.

Alarm tripped. Cyber security breach.

<No further details available>

He frowned. This didn't settle his concerns at all.

He connected a call with the AI lab.

"Sue? Is that you? What's going on down there?"

Sue's voice came through to his own audio implant. "Nothing... anymore. It all seemed to have settled down again," Sue reported back to him. "Probably just a sensor."

"It said it was a cyber breach," he added.

There was a pause on the line.

"Sue?" Lugdon said.

Sue's voice rang through the connection. "Ohhhhhh shit!" Her voice was serious.

"What?" he asked impatiently. "What is it?"

Sue's voice was hesitant. "I'm just pulling up the detailed report on the cyber alarm. It looks like it was tripped by the new bandwidth protocol."

"And?" he asked, not seeing the relevance.

Sue started talking quickly. "Well, it seems that there was a spike in processing power, tripping the alarm, but then it dropped, the alarm was canceled and then..." Her voice trailed off at a mutter.

"And then, what?" he asked again.

"Well," she explained, "it looks like the transfer of data out of the EtherTrak continued... but just underneath the threshold."

There was a pause on the line.

Sue was muttering to herself again. "It's almost as if there is a data transfer still happening."

Lugdon's mouth dropped open.

He immediately closed the call and nearly fell over scrambling for the door. He practically ran down the corridor back to the foyer where he had left Maya.

"Captain? Captain?" Sue called over the now closed connection. "Charming," she said going back to her work, muttering about the way these people treated her.

Lugdon practically flew down the corridors back to the foyer.

"Where did she go?" he demanded of the receptionist, his eyes searching everywhere. The receptionist, too bewildered to respond vocally, pointed at the door.

Lugdon was outside in an instant, looking frantically around the parking lot. He ran out and stopped in the middle of the road, looking it up and down, searching for the mysterious journalist whose visit had coincided with a massive download.

She was guilty. Of that he was *sure*.

But there was no one around. No buggy, no cars, no vehicles she could have taken. And no girl in high heels trotting down the road.

She was gone.

He'd been had, was his next thought, and the only question now was what to do about it.

He pulled up his holo to call the main gate as he ran back into the building.

Maya sat back in the pod, breathing a sigh of relief. "Thanks Emma. I had no idea how I was going to navigate back to the front gate. Especially not in these heels!"

"I had considered that your footwear was probably inappropriate for moving fast," Emma replied over the pod intercom.

"Yes, but totally appropriate to the mission." Maya responded. "Maybe."

She peered out of the pod window, watching the light outside turn into space as Emma jettisoned them up and beyond the stratosphere.

She replayed the moment again, remembering the excitement that had bubbled up in her as Emma guided her behind the building, how she had stomped up into the pod just in time for Emma to lift them up from the ground, the door still closing, so they were well above eye height by the time Lugdon had made it outside.

And once they were out of his view, Emma had carefully plotted a course through the blind spot around the side of the base in order for them to escape in their tiny pod, undetected by the base weapon system.

Maya sighed. "Great job Emma, really great job."

"You're welcome Maya," Emma responded. "I was glad to be of assistance."

"You know, next time I might rethink the high heels," Maya mused as Emma whisked them back off towards The Empress. "I wonder what Molly does…"

AI Lab, Nefertiti Military Research Facility, Ogg

Lugdon blustered into the lab, his voice reverberating from the walls. "Have Bob, or whatever he calls himself, track that woman who was just in my office with me!"

Sue spun around as Lugdon approached. "You mean Bourne?"

"Yes," Lugdon confirmed, disinterested in the name correction. "She must have gone somewhere and there isn't a place on this base that isn't covered with cameras."

Sue glanced anxiously about the lab. "Charles just popped out," she said.

"Well then get him back here!" Lugdon bellowed. Sue was sure he was about to explode, noticing a pulsing blood vessel on the side of his face now beet red.

She pulled up a holo and called Charles, and then hung up.

Moments later Charles came running in, flustered, his white lab coat billowing. "I'm here. Sorry. Sorry… What do you need, sir?"

Lugdon watched as Charles took up his seat at the console where he would talk with the AI. There was a white powder around Charles's face.

Probably donut residue, Lugdon assumed.

"Erm, Captain…" Charles started saying, slowly.

Lugdon was losing patience. "What?" he gruffed.

"You want Bourne to perform a task… the only problem is, Bourne isn't here anymore."

"What do you mean he isn't here. Where has he gone?"

"I've no idea. But there's nothing here. Not even a trace. He's disappeared."

Lugdon's face turned purple, then blue. He spoke very quietly, but there was no mistaking the anger and venom in his voice. "Find him, it, whatever he is, and find that girl. Whatever it takes."

Sue remained still as she watched the scene. Charles started typing furiously, trying to figure out where their pet AI had escaped to.

Lugdon disappeared, but called out, "You'll likely find the two together!" as he marched down the corridor.

Sue and Charles looked at each other. Charles suddenly had a look of recognition in his eyes. "He thinks the girl stole the AI!" he said excitedly.

Sue raised her eyes to the ceiling. "D'you think?" she asked sarcastically. "He's probably right, though. The timing was spot on." She mulled the information and began setting up the searches to track the girl from the moment she stepped onto the base to the moment she left.

CHAPTER FOURTEEN

<u>Bates Residence, Suburbs of Spire, Estaria</u>

"So how is the investigation going, dear?" Dr. Bates asked idly as he chopped some vegetables.

Carol turned around and picked up the dish of meat and popped it into the pre-heated oven. "The Molly Bates investigation?" she smiled. "Very well, I suppose. As far as investigations can go." She paused and put the oven gloves down on the counter. "Although I'm not too happy about what I've discovered."

Philip raised one eyebrow without looking up. "What's that then?"

Carol, finally permitted to talk about the discovery that had been weighing on her, took her apron off and whipped around to the other side of the counter. She poured herself a large glass of red wine and pulled up a screen on her wrist holo.

"What is it?" Philip asked, glancing up and then carefully returning his attention to the vegetables.

"This!" she told him, showing him a picture of Molly walking into one of the university buildings.

"What's that?" he asked unmoved. "A picture of Molly going into the university?"

"Yes, but look at her!" She pointed to the holoscreen floating in the air. "That leg wound is dripping so much blood she's going to bleed out if she doesn't get to a hospital."

Philip squinted. "When was this?" He asked.

"Three months ago." She replied.

He calmly cut through a white root. This particular vegetable could play hell with his sinuses if he didn't do this right. "Well then we know she survived it."

"That's not the point." She took a gulp of wine and pulled up the next picture. "This is her going into class with laser burns through her jacket. And look at her hair. She looks like she's been through an explosion. And yet... that's Joel dropping her off as if nothing has happened."

She sent the command for the next image. "And here... this is one from last week. Here you can see the other person in the pod is Sean. As in *Royale*..."

"Ah, yes!" Philip exclaimed as if she had just reminded him of nice brandy they had had once several years ago.

"Ah yes? Ah *yes*?" her voice raised an octave. "Do you *not* see what's going on here?"

Philip picked up the board of chopped vegetables and scraped them into a pan of water on the hob. "No... I suspect I'm missing what you're seeing."

Carol's expression was even more incredulous than it had been up to this point. "The point is, clearly, *your daughter* is working with some faction of the Federation. It looks like Royale is her handler. Or that Joel type... although we've not found anything to say he's Federation, but his record looks just too vanilla to be the truth."

Philip turned to look at his wife. "You mean, you think he's guilty of something because he's too straight? Or boring?"

"Yes," Carol agreed, twiddling the stem of the wine glass between two fingers. "Exactly that."

He turned the heat down just a bit, "Well, I still don't see why you're so upset."

Her mouth opened and closed a couple of times before she said, "Philip! Have you not been listening? Your daughter is probably an operative. For the Federation. Or worse. And she's under the command of that Royale beast."

Philip smiled.

"Why are you smiling?" She pressed, frustrated.

"I'm just pleased. I mean look at her," he said, pointing the knife at the holoscreens that lay about now that Carol had finished revealing her discovery. "She's a badass!"

Carol's mouth hung open this time, not closing at all.

"Oh, come on dear. Don't you think she can handle herself? After all, look, she's survived all that. She's clearly capable," he exclaimed.

Philip smiled to himself as he started tidying up the discarded vegetable matter.

"That's not the point," Carol scoffed, topping up her bulbous over-sized wine glass. "We decided long ago that we were going to shelter her from this life. That's why I worked so hard at getting promoted... so she would never find out what *we* were."

Philip glanced up at her as he wiped down the counter. "Right. Well, it looks like she was destined for the service whether she knew or not."

Carol's mouth suddenly stopped. She clamped her hand over her face and then froze, her gaze fixed. "You don't suppose she knows do you? They must have told her..."

Philip shrugged. "Might explain why it took her so long to talk to us again."

"Yes, but that started long ago. It had nothing to do with her disappearing in the first place."

"Maybe not, but I think Dr. Jones's theory about her feeling guilty about that incident is probably valid…"

"… in which case it was our fault she ran away. And it was because of our jobs."

"Now now Carol, there's no point in us torturing ourselves over it any more. What's done is done. It's all in the past."

Carol had begun sobbing quietly to herself. She took another gulp of wine. "I'm a terrible mother. I have no business being a mother any more… she was *right* to disappear."

Philip, who had heard this all a million times before, dried his hands off on the dish cloth and undid his own apron, leaving it on the side as he walked around to where his wife was sitting. He gently put his hand on her back and she turned into him, letting him hold her.

"How did it all go so wrong?" Carol sobbed, making his shirt tunic wet.

"It didn't go wrong. Like I said, she's turned out a real badass. What more could a parent want? A child who is confident and capable enough to do whatever *she chooses*."

There was a snot-curdling snort from against his chest where his wife was trying to compose herself.

"One that doesn't get into the same shit her parents got into!" she sobbed.

Philip patted her back as he spoke to her. "There, there. It's okay. If it's true and she is involved with the Federation, you can bet she's in it to fight the good fight. She never was one to sit back and watch injustice happen." He paused a moment before adding, "There may have been a certain inevitability around her career choice."

"Well," she huffed. "There are safer ways to make a difference in the world. Like that university job she has now."

Philip continued to stroke her back as the sobbing died down. "Yes. I mean, what could possibly be dangerous about educating the next generation of leaders in dangerously positive social policies."

He dryly raised his eyes to the ceiling, pretty certain the irony of his words would be lost on his wife.

As the crying ended, he peeled himself from her embrace, and poured some more wine into her glass. "I'm just going to change my shirt," he said, padding off to the bedroom. "Vegetables will need turning down in a few, too," he called out over his shoulder as he disappeared around a corner.

Carol pulled herself together and started closing up the holo-screens of Molly's surveillance.

Maybe the university was the safest place for her, she thought, wondering if there was a way to leverage her into staying with the university and giving up the Federation.

If there had been anything that Carol was naturally good at in her rise up the ranks, it was making sure that she could find the ways to maneuver people into doing what she wanted them to do.

Her daughter would not be an exception.

Gaitune-67, Molly's Conference Room

Pieter sat casually in Molly's conference room, his feet up on the chair next to him, enjoying the peace and quiet. As soon as he became aware of Molly striding through the door he straightened up, whipped his feet off the chair and nearly fell off onto the floor in the process. He caught his balance just in time.

"Hi!" he greeted her, sitting up, like he was trying to cover for something he'd been doing wrong.

Molly smiled, plonked herself down, and then swung her feet up on the chair next to her, just as Pieter had been sitting. She grinned at him, and he chuckled, awkwardly ruffling his hair. "So, erm… we've had Bourne uploaded into the base matrix, after Oz gave him some ground rules."

Molly frowned. "Ground rules?"

"Yeah," Pieter confirmed, "like respecting privacy, not taking over weapons systems, not being inappropriate with the comms and whatnot. Oh yeah… and no killing organics, or inorganics."

"I see."

Pieter grinned at her in his nerdy way. "Yeah, I think Emma had that last bit added in when he started probing the Empress."

"I'll bet she did!" Molly agreed. She paused a moment. "Goodness. Is it safe?"

Pieter looked confused by the question. "How do you mean?"

"I mean, is it safe… for Bourne to be let loose in the system?"

"Well, I… er, I don't know," he confessed, a little off guard. "I assume so. I guess. ADAM was supervising the upload, and I don't suppose he would have allowed it had he thought it wouldn't be."

"Okay," Molly agreed, making a mental note to have Oz check in with ADAM about the whole thing.

Joel walked in. "Wanna know the latest?"

"Sure," she answered, her voice qualifying the answer with an unspoken *maybe?*

"Oz has him watching files for cultural reference. Files like Ozzy Osbourne videos and music from the archives. He's actually been binge watching TV shows for the last several hours since he uploaded himself."

Molly frowned again. "Should we be worried how that might affect his development?"

Joel chuckled. "Words I never thought I'd hear Mommy Molly utter!" he chimed. "In my opinion, no. Though he'll probably end up with a weird-ass accent if it's anything like the shows you grew up on."

"Well, there is that," she agreed, raising one eyebrow playfully.

"What's more," Joel continued, pulling out the seat next to the one she had her feet on, "the General offered us the processing tech to allow him to upgrade and evolve his programming. He can even have a body if he wants."

Pieter leaned forward. "That would be interesting," he mused.

Molly nodded. "It would. And then he could be independent." She mulled the option.

Joel looked off into the distance, thinking about the prospect. "I wonder what he would want to do... with a body. And walking around with humans and stuff."

Molly sighed, slouching back in her chair. "I have no idea... I guess we can only wait and see."

"Hmm," Pieter said as he digested the idea. "Makes you wonder why they never offered that to Oz."

Molly glanced down at her hands, with no intention of responding. Joel sensed something and pushed her. "Molly?" he pressed.

She looked up at them both. "He did. When I was in the pod doc that time. He chose to stay."

Pieter's jaw dropped open. "Wow. I mean... *wow!*" he bumbled.

Joel looked at her in astonishment.

"Yeah," she said, bobbing her head gently looking back down at her hands.

"And Oz chose not to?" Joel pressed.

Molly took a deep breath, clearly biting back some emotion. "Yeah. He wanted to stay."

"Close to you," Joel said, finishing the thought she never could.

She bobbed her head again and then pulled up her holo. "Well, I suppose the next step is to float the idea with Oz and let them talk it through."

Joel knew the subject was now closed, and that he was being dismissed. He pushed his chair out and got to his feet. "I'll get right on it," he confirmed. He glanced over at Pieter, who was equally shocked by the revelation, and then headed out of the door.

· · ·

Storage cupboard, Skóli Uppstigs Academy, Spire, Estaria

Team Kurns found themselves back in the privacy of the Level Three storage room, with only their holo light to illuminate their conversation.

Giles arrived just a moment before and was fiddling with his belongings, trying to place them on a shelf where he could find them again in the blackness.

Eventually he turned around to address the group, a small flashlight his only illumination. "Okay, folks," he whispered into the darkness. There was a distinct feel of the theater between the darkness and the lit-up professor.

"Here's what we know," he said. "Our classroom was smoke-bombed by three little twerps with questionable ideologies. They were recruited to disrupt things at the university by Arnold Sloth. What *I* want to know is why? How he found them and what their end game is."

He glanced around the half light and shadows to see the figures taking notes or listening attentively.

"This is where we want the investigation to go and our first step to finding all this out is what?"

He waited expectantly for a response.

"Finding out everything about Arnold Sloth." It was Cleavon's voice.

"Correct!" Giles confirmed. "So how did we get on?"

Cleavon stood up from the stack of boxes he'd been perched on. "Arnold Sloth. Forty-three. Never mated. Graduated from Ogg University top of his class. Set up shop on his own as a fixer, straight out of college, but then closed it down five years later when he went off grid."

"Do we know why?" Giles asked into the darkness.

Cleavon flicked to another holoscreen. "There was a case that he was a material witness in. The court documents have been sealed, though..."

Giles quickly said, "Get hold of them."

"But it's on *Ogg*," Cleavon protested.

Giles smiled, the shadows cast from the angle of the holo lights making his face look demonic. "Would that be a problem for a hacking genius?" he asked.

Cleavon looked down at his holo. "No sir. I... I'll get right on it."

"Okay, what else do we have?"

It was Soraya's turn. "I tracked his communications. Managed to get into one of his holos. He has a few burners I think. For the most part, he is using some device that seems to re-route his call signals through various places and servers, but I've been able to untangle about 18 percent of his communications since we got his name. He's been in touch with this institution twice."

Soraya pulled up a holoscreen with an image of a company. Some kind of family office.

Giles started reading off the site: "Northern Clan of Cambodian."

He cast his gaze around at the others. "Okay, what do we know about this office?"

Raza injected herself into the show and tell. "Only that they want to maintain the status quo of the Central Systems. In terms of education they make big donations to institutions who have more traditional values. They also have holdings in certain medical facilities, research, pharmaceuticals, not to mention the regulatory bodies of the financial sector."

Giles stroked his chin as he listened. "Well, this is a red flag if ever there was one. If we can find out why they want to disrupt the university we get closer to finding out what their end game is. And therefore...?"

Soraya answered, needlessly raising her hand excitedly. "What we need to do to protect ourselves or neutralize the threat."

Giles snapped his fingers and pointed at her. "Exactly. You're getting it."

Elroy pipped up from the darkness a little further back. "So...

what's our next move?" he asked.

Rhodez saw his opportunity to demonstrate initiative. "I'll run down the numbers. If I can get into their holo system, we can find out who else is involved and maybe even narrow this down to an individual in the organization."

"Great," Giles replied. "Soraya, you stay on the Sloth holo. Do what you can. It's all useful data." He looked out at the outline of the group against the darkness. "And above all else — what's our rule Number One?"

"No one talks about fight club?" That was Ake, who hadn't spoken all session.

There were a few smiles and looks of recognition in the room. Clearly some of them had done their research.

Giles smiled. "And rule Number Two?"

"Refer back to rule Number One," Dhashana piped up enthusiastically from the shadows.

Giles wagged his finger in the direction of her voice in acknowledgment. "Yeah, but this is more important than double scoring rule one. Rule two is - for the love of all that is holy — Don't. Get. Caught."

His face was serious as he looked at each of the faces in the storage cupboard - or at least where he thought they were from the dim reflections of holo light. "Not least," he added, "because it will be my pretty head on the chopping block with the Mollster if anything were to escalate. Capisce?"

There were mutters of comprehension and agreement

"Okay. Great. Class dismissed," he said as he turned off his flashlight.

Clandestine Operations HQ, Spire

"Ma'am?"

"Yes, Roberts?" Carol Bates strode over to look over her associates shoulder. He had three screens laid out. One large one in the center, and one to each side of him. He pointed to the holoscreen to his left.

"That is the scorecard for our typical efforts," he told her and she nodded. Effectively, seventy percent effective, twenty percent neutralized and ten percent either blocked or worse, blocked and an effort to trace where it started.

He punched a couple of keys and the screen changed. "This is our effort for this project."

He didn't need to point anything out to Carol. Her eyes opened wide when she saw nothing her team had done so far had been effective, twenty percent were neutralized and *eighty* percent of the attacks had either counter-attacks or all out traces that meant a full-on defense with a massive amount of counter-hacking was going on.

They had kicked over a leergong's nest.

Shit! Carol stormed towards her office. This was the last thing she needed. She had promised Philip that Molly would never find out.

And now she was about to find out.

And if that weren't bad enough, she couldn't decide which was going to be worse, Molly finding out it was her own mother prying into her business, or that she would be thinking she was under attack.

"Ma'am?" Another well-manicured Estarian strode up to her.

"Yes, Wigglesworth?"

"Ma'am, Dr. Bates is here to see you."

"*Fuuuuck,*" she muttered under her breath. "Okay, let him through," she sighed.

"Ma'am, he doesn't have proper clearance anymore," he replied.

Carol's eyes narrowed in surprise. "Yes yes, I'm well aware of that. But do you know who he is?"

Wigglesworth stood a bit straighter, "Yes Ma'am. Only one of the best operatives this office has ever seen."

"One of? Don't let him hear you saying that." Carol answered, a smile on her face, a shake of her head imagining the result of that conversation.

He bowed. "Yes ma'am. I'll go fetch him now."

"Thank you, Wigglesworth."

He disappeared only to return several minutes later with her husband.

"Hello, dear," Dr. Bates said from the doorway. He nodded to Wigglesworth, who bowed slightly and took his leave.

He glanced over at what was in Carol's hand, then turned and closed the door. "Thought you'd be needing me right about now," he said, a little smugness in his voice.

Carol tapped the end of the cigarette on the old fashioned cigarette case. She rummaged in her desk drawer for her lighter and lit up.

Philip sat down in her visitor's chair. "That bad?" he asked.

She nodded, taking another long drag of the cigarette. She held the smoke in her lungs for several seconds before slowly exhaling into the air ahead of her, watching the smoke disappear into the air conditioning extraction fans. "She's going to find out," she said bluntly.

Philip clasped his hands. He nodded his head gently, biding his time until his opinion was asked for.

"We've tripped some kind of protocol when we were looking into her Federation links," Carol added after a moment.

Philip frowned. "So you may have tipped off the Federation. Not Molly."

"No - if it were a Federation trip wire we wouldn't have tripped it. We know their signature moves. We would have spotted it," she said.

Philip remained quiet.

"Anyway, she's going to find out, or right now she's running a code red, panicking for no reason."

Philip had a twinkle in his eye. "I wouldn't say for no reason."

Carol looked confused.

"Well, it is Carol Bates who is hunting her down… only the best in the business." He winked at her.

Carol wasn't amused. She took another drag of her cigarette, the frustration showing as a tightness around her mouth as she inhaled.

Philip filled the silence this time. "So what's your play?" he asked.

Her gaze became fixed on a point on the floor of her windowless office. "I don't know. Yet. Clearly we need another way in."

Philip smiled. She said 'we'. He knew immediately what that meant. In that moment he was glad he had taken the gamble and went downtown to drop in on his wife. She was nothing if not predictable.

At least to him.

"So you need intel about the Federation," he clarified slowly. "So you need someone who can give you that intel."

His days as an operative were shining through. Operatives developed assets. Assets were people in this business. And people can tell you anything you needed to know.

He watched her carefully, waiting for her to reveal a tell. "But why would they give you anything?" he probed.

She sighed and pulled her gaze from the floor to look at him. "Because they are meant to be back-door allies?" she posited. "Because it's my daughter." Her voice trembled. This had rattled her. He could tell.

He tried another tact. "Have they even admitted that Royale works for them?"

"Nope," she confirmed. "Not ever in the thirty years since we first encountered him."

"And yet you're considering approaching him now."

"Yes," she said.

"And what makes you think that he'll admit anything to you?"

"Because I have evidence of him and their secret ops…"

Philip cut in. "Which he knows you can never use to out him."

Carol was determined. "And a secret weapon," she added firmly.

"Oh yeah? What's that?" he asked, almost impressed.

"Not what… Who," she corrected him.

Philip's eyes were bright as he leaned forward in his chair. "Are you going to let me in on it then?"

"No way," she smiled, regaining her chutzpah. "Not this time. This is need-to-know only, hubby dearest."

Philip knew there was no point in pressing further. They'd all been taught to withstand all kinds of torture and duress. He uncrossed his legs and got to his feet, zipping up the upper part of his atmosjacket.

"Well then," he said turning towards the door. "I suppose I'll see you tonight."

Carol nodded and waved to him. "Yes dear. But thank you for stopping by. It was good to have someone to talk to."

Dr. Bates smiled to her. "Any time, my love." And with that he disappeared out of her office with the same air and grace as he always carried himself around those offices. He was legend amongst the analysts. They all knew that. And he knew it too.

Carol sighed, cigarette still in hand, and started searching her holo for a certain encrypted file she needed for her next move.

CHAPTER FIFTEEN

Gaitune-67, Kitchen
Molly strode into the kitchen, grabbed a mug and walked to the dispenser for a bit of hot water. She looked over at Paige, who was working at the kitchen table.

"Where's Maya?"

Paige looked up, and saw that Molly's face was a little more blank than usual. "Working on something with Pieter I think. You okay?"

Molly nodded, "Yeah, all good. You?"

Still trying to see if she could get any tells from her boss, Paige said, "Yeah. Just plugging on."

Molly... we have a problem.

What? What is it?

It seems that someone is still probing, looking for you.

Well it can't be Bourne, he knows where I am. It must be Lugdon and his team of preppy war hungry imbeciles.

No it's not Bourne. Or the research facility.

Well who then?

We... don't know.

Just then, Pieter and Maya came crashing into the kitchen, their faces tense.

"Oz just told me," Molly explained before they could blurt out what was happening.

She placed her cup down on the table. "What we need to make sure first and foremost is can we shut down their attacks?"

Pieter tilted his head. "Well... they're not really attacks," he confessed. "If anything, it's more that they're pinging our defenses and trying to test where our vulnerabilities are. They're looking for intel and to build up a map of our assets. They're not attacking yet."

Maya pulled a chair out and plonked herself down at the table. "If anything," she admitted, "it would be easier to catch them if they were mounting a full on attack. But as it is it's like trying to catch a ghost."

Molly leaned against the counter. "Okay, what are our options?" she asked.

"Well," Pieter began, thinking on his feet. "I think we can probably go back through some data and cross reference any spiders or pings which have hit us with the one that just tripped our protocol. At least then we'll know that this isn't just an accidental hit, and with a bit of luck we might be able to build up a picture of what they are targeting."

Molly nodded her head once. "Okay. Do it."

She turned to Maya and raised an eyebrow. "I suppose I could reach out to Lugdon and ask him." Maya answered.

Paige chuckled. "I know, why don't you call him and ask him out on a date! See if you can pump him for information?"

Maya chuckled, but then realised that Molly was serious. She cleared her throat and returned to the task in hand. "No... erm... seriously, what I was thinking was getting into his computer and seeing if it might have been his team. Once through the firewall, I could poke around and be in and out without him feeling a thing."

Paige sniggered.

Molly glanced at her and then moved on. "Do it," she confirmed to Maya.

"Oz?" She called out to the all hearing AI.

"Yup?" He responded on the intercom.

"Any suggestions?"

"Yes, I'll help them both with the pieces of their suggestions they can't do without me. I'm sure one of those avenues will show up something."

"Okay, great. Make it so," Molly said, smiling encouragement at her team of nerds. She picked up her hot water and strode out of the door.

She hadn't gone three paces before she heard Maya giggling and chastising Paige for being such a kid in front of the boss.

Molly took a moment and smiled to herself. There was no doubt about it. She was their boss now. And acting like it was good for the team, even if she felt she was missing out on some of the social aspects of being one of the crew.

She sighed and headed back to her conference room knowing one more problem was on her plate, but also being handled by the best team she could ever hope for.

Skóli Uppstigs Academy, Spire, Estaria

The Sark was high in the sky as Professor Giles Kurns strode down the corridor to his first lecture of the day. It had been a good morning: his mocha was just right, he'd had an easy trip into his office, and all was right with the world.

Then he saw Molly Bates, action heroine extraordinaire, most popular lecturer and founder of the university.

Also known as "Boss".

"Morning!" he called brightly, determined not to let his good mood be spoiled by feelings of inadequacy.

"Morning!" Molly called back, flashing her million-credit

smile as she marched from the other end of the corridor towards her classroom, which adjoined his.

She hovered by the door before she went in. Hand on handle, she turned to him as he approached. "All okay since I was away?"

"You were away?" Giles asked, quickly scanning his memory in case there was something he needed since she was right there.

"Yeah. You were going to cover my morning lecture?" she asked.

Dammit. Rumbled. Giles thought.

"Oh right. Yes," he responded. Had he not had his arms full of books he would have been grabbing for his glasses right now.

Molly narrowed one eye at him. "Giles?" she said in a low voice so that passing students couldn't hear her. "You *didn't miss it* did you?"

Giles straightened up, taking a deep breath to own it. "Yes. Yes I did. But I *have* a good reason."

"The smoke bomb incident?" she asked.

"Yes." He replied.

She pursed her lips. "Hmm, I heard about that from Oz."

Giles waited for her next words.

"Great work," she said, flashing that smile again.

Giles felt his heart miss a beat... and then his chest swell. "Thank you!" he uttered, his voice catching in his excitement.

"Anything else I should know?" she asked almost *too* casually.

Giles hesitated, wondering if now was really the best time to be fessing up to using student labor to hunt down the threat to the university, which she also didn't know about. "Erm. No. Nothing yet. But... let's catch up over the weekend or something. Have a chat?"

Molly smiled, taking her hand from the door handle to allow a straggler into the class ahead of her. "Okay. Sounds good."

She moved to catch the door before it swung closed and stepped inside.

"Great!" Giles said as cheerfully as he could. "I'll see you later.

Got to be in class." He pointed at his classroom door which had been opened by one of the students.

Molly just smiled and let the door shut, disappearing behind the door.

Giles, still reeling from the emotional roller coaster that was the last ten seconds, gathered his thoughts and focused down to the task at hand. He took a deep breath and stepped over the threshold ready to do battle to convince his class that even though he wasn't hipster Estarian-cool, he was still worth paying attention to.

No sooner was he in front of the class than an applause erupted.

Oh good lord! he exclaimed, placing his teaching materials down on the front bench and looking around the classroom. First, he noticed the windows had been covered, awaiting repair. As he settled into the overwhelming feeling of his class applauding him, he realized why.

Soraya stood up. "Professor Kurns, on behalf of the class I would like to say thank you for keeping us safe from the smoke bombers." She smiled brightly, and if Giles didn't know any better he suspected she was perhaps even flirting.

"And for pursuing them after the fact, too." She winked as another applause rang through the class. Of course, she was publicly referring to giving chase to the bombers.

But privately, she was referring to the little secret society they had going on.

Giles, his hands now free, removed his glasses and started cleaning them again. "Thank you Soraya," he said graciously, and then nodded regally to the class.

"Thank you, everyone. Now let's turn to page 238 in your strategy textbooks and pick up on the Cantopole Wars case study again…"

Molly stepped into her classroom. The hubbub quickly died down as students scrambled to their desks and fixed their attention on Molly.

Molly unzipped her atmosjacket and stepped up to the front bench, pulling up a holoscreen of her teaching notes. Out of her peripheral vision she clocked a smartly dressed gentleman, too old to be one of her students, sitting patiently in the back of the class.

Who's the guy at the back?

Rick Shadrows is his name. It's some regulatory body representative that Garett Atkins suggested we humor. You ok'd it last week.

You mean in that string of things you asked me about during my workout?

You said you could multitask.

I did. And I can. I remember now.

Good. So I don't need to call security on his ass.

No. In fact, it will give me a good opportunity to see if I can get a read on him.

Ahh, with your hoodoo voodoo energy reading thing.

Exactly. And don't call it that. When you say hoodoo I think of Paige's granny growing herbs in her back yard.

Roger that.

She started her lecture. "Okay, we're onto the second phase of the Estarian unification convention. Who can tell me what the primary concerns were when the parties sat down to negotiate?"

Two hands went up. One was Donovan, her mousey-haired medical monitor.

The other was the gentleman at the back of the room.

Molly smiled at him as she moved out from behind the front bench and stepped off the platform to be closer to her students. "Class, we have a guest joining us today. Please say hello to Mr. Rick Shadrows."

The class turned their attention on the man and said their hellos.

Mr. Shadrows nodded and smiled politely, acknowledging the sentiment.

"Mr. Shadrows is here to observe to make sure that we're following regulations. I'm sure he'll probably want to ask you some questions..." She looked at him as if to give him permission. "So please cooperate and treat him with the same respect you'd treat any faculty member."

There were grunts and murmurs of acknowledgment.

"So, Mr. Shadrows. You had your hand up to answer the question," she ventured.

Shadrows nodded. "Yes. I believe you're referring to the circumstances that led up to the Huntington Convention, which created the unification of the two major powers on Estaria. In essence, the major considerations were how much trade each party could bring to the table and how much aid each would supply to its relative populations in terms of reparations."

Molly nodded. "Anything else?"

"Well, there were a few rumors that there were some back door dealings between a couple of their major corporations at the time, but those were wholly unsubstantiated and probably started by rebels within the two groups to try and undermine the terms that were eventually reached."

Molly kept her expression friendly but blank, noticing certain students in the class recognizing the paradigm the intruder was answering with. "And Mr. Shadrows, were these claims ever upheld down the line?"

"Actually yes, but by that time the corporations in question had been dissolved and..."

She wasn't paying attention to the rest of his argument. She'd heard it several times before over the years. She had already started moving back to her desk on the raised platform. "Right," she agreed as she pulled up a holoscreen and pushed it against the wall for the whole class to see.

"Here are the names of the executives associated with those two corporations... the ones charged and found guilty of policy manipulation, extortion and bribery, I believe the exact charges were."

She flicked the screen and a second set of data was displayed next to the first.

"And here are the names of two new companies which then incorporated within eighteen months following," she told the class as they took in the new data on the screen.

There were murmurs in the class.

"So what can we conclude from this data?" she asked.

Most of the hands in the class went up.

Molly nodded at one of the quieter students who rarely raised his hand. "Yes, Nathan?"

Nathan cleared his throat and quietly explained the case as he saw it, including the fact that it looked like the companies just renamed themselves to get out of trouble.

Molly nodded. "That's certainly one theory," she agreed, allowing space for other interpretations of the data.

She looked to the back row of the class, "Anything to add to that assessment, Mr. Shadrows?"

"Ah well..." The man looked embarrassed. "Yes, I can see that is a potentially valid point now."

There was a snigger from the front of the class that Molly silenced with the glare. She continued the lesson.

Eventually, part-way through a discourse on the third phase of the development, the bell rang, releasing both Molly, the observer, and the class from the inconvenient contentions of education.

The class filtered out, realizing that after-class stories of rogue missions and near-death assignments were probably out of the question while Mr. Shadrows was around.

The mysterious gentleman waited for the last of them to filter out, and cautiously approached the front of the class and nodded. "I have to say, Ms. Bates, I was expecting something quite different when I came here."

She watched him approach the last few steps. "Oh. Yes?"

He nodded his head slowly a few times. "Yes. I thought things would be a little less... rigorous," he admitted.

"Well, I can understand that concern, Mr. Shadrows. But if we're going to shape change, then we have to do it from a solid foundation of facts and careful, considered evaluation, no?" she left her question hanging.

His earlier nods started to become more pronounced. "Yes, yes, I agree." The man's eyes lit up. He stuck his hand out to shake with Molly. She reached out and took it. "I'm going to reflect nothing but good things in my report."

Molly could sense that he was genuine, despite his original feelings when she had first stepped into the room. Her grindle senses had picked up that he was indeed there to start the process of shutting them down, but now, shaking his hand and seeing his enthusiasm for their work, she didn't pick up a trace of it at all.

"I'm very happy to hear that Mr. Shadrows."

"Please, call me Rick!" He chirped.

She carefully didn't raise an eyebrow. "Ok, Rick." She repeated.

"Well," he said moving towards the door. "I'll be in touch if I need anything else. But thank you very much for your time."

Molly smiled, waving to him as he walked away. "Excellent. Yes, please do. Thank you Rick!"

And with that he disappeared out of the door and down the corridor.

What was that?

What was what?

You know what.

I don't.

Well, he came in with one set of beliefs and left with another. Don't think I didn't hear you logging in your mind what you were picking up about his state emotionally.

You noticed how easily he changed his mind?

Yes.

And you know that most people would point to the information and say that that was what changed his mind, right?

Yes. And they would be wrong. There have been countless studies that have shown that information had very little effect on someone's opinion. Most people will simply reject it, diminish it or disregard it in order to maintain their current paradigm.

This is also true.

So something else changed his mind.

You're back to that then.

I think it's worth looking into. Apart from anything, if this creates long term changes in peoples' beliefs then imagine the impact that could have on our missions? Heck on the Federation.

Yes, and imagine the ethical issues with that too. It wouldn't be any different from hacking someone's code, methinks.

Hmm. There is that.

So, how are we getting on with finding out who has been probing us?

I'm still working on it.

Should I be worried?

No. Why?

Because whoever these people are who are trying to find out about us have so far evaded you. You're the most powerful AI this system has seen.

Molly paused, weighing her next words to Oz.

I don't suppose we need to bring in ADAM to help do we?

No. I've got this. I'm just having difficulty, what with having to help Bourne and the missions and...

Ah. Single parenthood catching up to you eh?

Well, I didn't think I was on my own in this...

You're not. Molly chuckled. *I just liked the expression. It seems to map to the challenge you're having.*

What challenge?

You know — balancing your career and child rearing.

Oz went quiet.

Oz?

Yes?

You okay?

Yes, sorry. I was, erm... just contemplating the dilemma. I'm wondering if there is a way of increasing my capacity...

Well, let me know if I can help.

I will.

And if you need ADAM on this, then let's be smart about it. It's perfectly okay to ask for help.

Hmm. Okay.

Molly could sense his pride was stopping him, but figured she should let him run a little longer to see if he came to the conclusion himself. She wanted him to make the decision. Not for her to dictate it to him.

She picked up her jacket and headed out of the classroom.

Outside University, carport

The Sark was setting as Rick made his way across the half-built carport of the new university. The campus grounds were still in disarray in places, but it seems that a big injection of cash had been made to smarten certain areas up.

The college administrator, Garett Atkins, had given him a tour earlier that day and pointed out where the various tech labs and discussion theaters were going to be developed as soon as they had the head count to justify it.

"Hi, yes, I'm here," he said to his holo connection.

Rick had been on hold and the holocall connected just as he

was arriving at his car and began a battle with getting in with his jacket and case.

"Yes sir. It went very well… and honestly I know we were looking for signs of impropriety, but I couldn't find anything observable."

He listened.

"Yes. Yes. I understand that. But we can't find something *that isn't there.*"

An air of frustration descended on his good mood.

Shadrows was silent as he listened to the voice on the other end of the line. He got into his car and closed the door, hoping that the noise canceling algorithm would filter out the bang.

"Yes, I'll do that, of course sir, but I don't think this warrants further investigation. Everything seems to be in order. Yes. Thank you sir. I will."

And with that the call was disconnected.

Rick sat in the quiet of his car, contemplating what he'd just seen over the course of the day. He had been convinced that this outfit was spelling social trouble and that it would cause a problem in the future. But since Molly's class, and seeing how she was instructing the students to think for themselves and not take hearsay at face value… there was something valuable there.

And try as he might, he couldn't seem to recapture the feelings he had felt earlier that day about the whole thing.

He started the car and buckled his harness.

Well, if his boss wanted his report, he'd just have to accept it as he saw it, he concluded, pulling out of the car port and heading off for the stratohighway.

But right now, he needed a beer.

CHAPTER SIXTEEN

Undisclosed bar, Spire

Carol Bates looked up from her holo as the waiter passed by her table on the way to the next. She glanced at the ice in her drink and then at the time on her holoscreen.

Her asset was late.

She glimpsed over at the man at the next table. He'd come in a few seconds after she had, so naturally he was suspect.

She turned her attention back to the screening reports from her team from the data they had captured before she shut the operation down. She hoped there might be a clue in there. Something to give her insight into what her daughter was doing with Sean Royale.

So far she'd turned up nothing.

Just then a pretty young Estarian female came in through the front door. She was all made up, but dressed casually. She glanced around, her eyes still adjusting to the dim light of the bar.

A second later she spotted Carol and headed straight over.

Carol stood up and signaled to the seat on the other side of the booth. "Glad you could make it, Karina," Carol said, with the air of forced pleasantries.

Karina looked at her sternly. "You didn't give me much choice. Seems I'm at your beck and call these days."

Carol pursed her lips together and lowered her eyes. Her demeanor was no-nonsense, but she didn't want to come across as domineering or harsh. "I understand that might be how you feel," she said quietly.

The waiter came over and Karina ordered before returning to the conversation. "So... why am I here?" she asked, crossing her legs and sitting back in the booth.

"I need you for a job," Carol said flatly.

Karina's interest was piqued. "What kind of job? Engage and neutralize? Engage and interrogate?"

"Engage and marry," Carol answered.

Karina's mouth dropped open. "You're not serious?"

"I am."

"Who's the target."

"We'll come to that."

"What's the purpose?"

"Information, mostly. But then once you're in we might need to leverage your position, so you'll want to go in with a long-term plan."

"How long-term."

"Maybe a few years."

Karina started choking, coughing on her surprise.

"Oh, come on," Carol remarked. "It's not like you haven't done anything like this before."

"Well, I've never actually gone through with the marriage part. At least not for work."

Carol sipped her limeade. "Well, first time for everything. It will look great on your resume."

Karina's eyes tensed up as she processed what she was going to have to do. Just then her drink arrived. No sooner had the server set it on the table she picked it up and downed it.

"Another," she said, signaling to the server, who had only seconds before moved away from the table.

Carol continued. "You will of course be compensated. Usual rate for a long term gig."

Karina nodded, still stunned. "And the target?" she asked.

Carol sat back in her chair. "Yes. That's something else you'll have to acclimatize to."

"Why, who is it?" She asked, her face suddenly a little more animated. "You've not landed me some prince from one of the provinces have you? Is that why I got it? Because of the human thing?"

Carol raised one eyebrow, pretty much in the same way her daughter would when casting doubt on a statement.

"You know," Karina said, her eyes dancing now as she shrugged her shoulders from side to side. "All the Estarian princes like humans. That's why they keep marrying them."

Carol felt her inward face role her eyes. Her poker face remained unchanged. "No Karina. It's not an Estarian prince... although, some people have called him a prince among men... over the years."

Karina's eyes narrowed as she tried to piece together the clues she was being given.

"It's Sean Royale," Carol finally admitted.

"My EX?" She hissed.

"Yes. Your ex." Carol replied calmly.

"And you thought this would be a good idea because?"

Just then Karina's second drink arrived, reminding her to keep her voice down. She visibly shrank and waited for the server to move away again.

Once he was out of earshot, she got back to their conversation. "You've got to be kidding me!"

"I can assure you I'm not."

Karina's eyes roamed the bar before she asked, "And you can't send anyone else?"

Carol shook her head, "No. We need the history. The relationship."

"And *you* think that after everything that's happened in the past, I'll still be able to play him?" Karina asked.

"Yes," Carol answered.

Karina slumped back in the booth again, her face twisted like a teenager in discourse with a parent.

"You're the only one who can do this," Carol added, again trying to make it look like she wasn't strong-arming her.

But then, they both knew that Karina had no choice, and any illusion that she might have was merely a formality to make proceedings feel civilized.

Karina downed her drink and placed the empty glass back on the table in front of her. "Okay. When do I make my play?"

"I'll send you the details, but basically this is how it's going to play out…" Carol began.

The two women occupied the booth for another twenty minutes, ordering another round of drinks. Carol left a reasonable tip when she paid the bill and quietly left the bar a good ten minutes after Karina departed. With Karina now in play, her plan to find out what her daughter was really up to would have a longer shelf life than the digitally driven assignments.

Gaitune-67, Molly's Conference Room

"Hey."

Sean popped his head in to the conference room, tapping his knuckle against the door.

"I heard about what happened today," he told her.

Molly didn't turn around or look up. "With what?" she asked, distracted.

Sean stepped into the room and stood in front of her, just behind her line of vision on her holo. "With the shady guy coming into your class," he qualified. "Oz was monitoring his communications after he came out. Seems he had a change of heart about coming after you."

"I didn't know he was coming after me," she lied.

"He was. And now he's not." Sean remained motionless.

"Well, that's good then," she replied.

"It can be," he agreed skeptically. "But I think this is a new skill you've developed."

Molly looked up from her holoscreen, giving Sean her full attention. She continued to play dumb. "You mean, persuading douchebags not to give me a hard time? Or you mean my charisma and charm?"

"Ha!" Sean snorted. "The charisma and charm you can keep. But I think there is a realm walking thing going on too. I spoke to Arlene a—"

"You spoke to Arlene without talking to me first?"

"Yes. I did. I had to be sure I wasn't crazy. She thinks that it might be another skill you've acquired since you've been going through those... changes."

Molly frowned, concentrating on the new information. "You mean the ascension process?"

"Right. Changes."

Molly raised one eyebrow at him skeptically. "I'm assuming there is a point to this conversation."

"There is," he agreed, speaking more swiftly now. "If you're able to affect peoples' decisions, then you're a risk to the Federation. Until we figure out what this is, and how you can control it, we can't have you anywhere near the General... or anyone else in command."

Molly paused for a moment. "In case I change their minds?" she asked slowly.

"Yes. Exactly." He pulled out a seat and sat down a few seats over from her.

"Shit," she muttered under her breath.

"So," Sean continued, "that means no more trips up to the

ArchAngel. And no more missions until Arlene has had a chance to investigate further."

Molly's frown only deepened. "You mean you're grounding me?"

"Yes. For your own good... as well as everyone else's."

"I'm not sure you have that authority."

"I will when I talk to the General about this", he said firmly. "And just one more thing..."

Sean paused, as if searching for the words. "Since you can almost push your will onto anyone... I'd be careful around even your team... in case you accidentally push them into doing something they don't want."

Molly regarded Sean carefully as she eased back in her chair, allowing one leg to slip out from underneath her and onto the floor. "So, if I'm able to push my will... what's to stop me from changing your mind right now?"

Sean's face dropped and the color drained from his face. "Nothing," he said quickly, looking flustered.

Suddenly he was on his feet again.

She looked at him bewildered.

"I have to go," he told her, then disappeared out of the door.

She listened as his footsteps hurried away down the corridor.

Was that weird, or was that just me?

I think that was weird. Want me to find out what that was all about.

Yeah... if you can. Well, hang on. How would you?

I'd ask him.

No no nooooo! Leave it. I don't want anymore awkward conversations. It was likely nothing. Let it go.

Ok, you're the boss, Boss. Wow - did I just agree to that because that was your will?

Shut up, Oz.

Shutting up.

Ooops. Look. Maybe you did it again...

Molly rolled her eyes and settled back into her work. Things were getting weird around here, and if there were more effects from her rebirth, then she'd just have to deal with them.

Later.

Outside Molly's conference room

Sean stepped out of the conference room and headed back into the main safe house.

He needed to talk to the General.

Stat.

Just then, his holo blipped. He looked down. It was a message from an unknown designation.

He poked at the display and the message came up as a video. He headed down the corridor waiting for it to load. He poked a holo function making sure the audio was connected to his implant.

As the first frame appeared he glanced down at it and his eyes nearly popped out of his head.

Then he ran smack into the corridor double doors. "Fuck!" He recoiled aware of the thwack across his head and knee but completely distracted by the video.

"Hi, baby!" It was Karina's voice. The voice he thought he'd never hear again. The lilting voice of a damsel in distress which got him tied up in all kinds of trouble back in his younger days. And the one that came to represent nothing but pain and despair.

His thoughts froze.

"I know we agreed we wouldn't talk again, but this is serious. I don't have anyone else I can call and I really need your help. I don't think I have long. They're going to find me. Hell, I just hope they can't trace this message..."

Her voice trailed off as her eyes flicked to something off camera.

Sean squinted at the video render, trying to see where she

might be and what was going on. He clocked the backdrop. She was in a room, probably on a ship, judging by the background and the life support plumbing and gubbins in the ceiling.

"Please, call me back. I know we left things badly... but... you're my last hope." She smiled a weak, half smile. Her lip wobbled.

And then the image was gone.

The message ended.

Sean's heart beat hard. He felt a lump in his throat and a kind of terror that sent adrenaline through his whole artificially enhanced system. For a second he couldn't think of where he was going or what he was doing.

And he *needed* to think.

He turned around and headed back down the corridor to his quarters. If Karina was calling him on this number it meant that she was in danger.

Life and death kind of danger.

After all, that was their agreement.

That was how they were both going to exist in the same galaxy... making sure their paths never crossed again.

Unless the unthinkable had happened.

And by the sounds of her message, it had.

CHAPTER SEVENTEEN

Giles's office, Level 3, Main Building, Skóli Uppstigs Academy
Hans Duo stood just inside the door to Giles's office.

He wore a beat-up atmosuit that had the odd tear in it around the seals. His boots were scuffed and had smudges of oil and dirt, the kind one only picks up by being around empty warehouses and abandoned buildings these days, in these parts. Despite, that he had managed to find a clean undershirt and comb his hair, which still lay in a haphazard fashion framing his face.

"Ah, here it is," Giles said, pointing at a screen on his desk holo. He turned a second holo frame towards Hans and pushed it forward. The boy ventured further into the office squinting to see the holoscreen. He took hold of the frame and expanded it out to read, his eyes darting quickly from side to side.

"Pop your holo number in there," Giles instructed, wagging his finger in a downward motion indicated that Hans should scroll down.

The boy did as he was told. He shook his head in amazement, realizing that throwing a smoke bomb through the classroom window might actually result in him receiving the formal education he had previously been denied. The concept was practically mind-boggling to him.

Giles had turned his attention to transmitting the files once he had the address. He glanced up briefly as he worked. "And did you tell the police everything when you went back?"

"Yes, sir."

"Good," he grunted, returning his eyes to his holo. "Honesty is always the best policy."

"With respect, sir," Hans corrected, "that's not why you had me do it."

"Oh?" Giles leaned idly back in his desk chair, regarding the boy skeptically.

"You had me tell the detective who hired me so that he could trace him back to his boss and put pressure on them while you took a run at them through some other angle, increasing the stakes for them so they'll eventually slip up." Hans's eyes glimmered with the cockiness of youth as he hit return on the holoscreen and passed it back to the professor.

Giles finalized the file transfer to the boy's holo and rocked back in his chair again. "Very good," he drawled slowly, his tone mildly impressed.

Hans grinned cheekily. "Your students aren't the only ones who study the ways of the Sanguine Squadron." Hans tried to keep his tone balanced and face straight. He wasn't fooling Giles though. Giles could see he was enjoying his moment as a smart-ass.

Giles raised his chin slightly as he regarded his new student. "I'm surprised you can find enough intel on them. The Squadron, that is," he remarked, subtly fishing.

"Oh, you'd be surprised," Hans said, excitedly walking right into Giles's set up. "There are a number of blogs which publish some of the stories your classes are told…"

Bingo.

Giles sat up, his face darkening. "By our own students?"

"Yes, sir."

Giles rubbed his chin slowly as he regarded his source. "Interesting," he mumbled, making a mental note to raise it with Molly.

The conversation lulled for a moment before Giles snapped his attention back to Hans. "Well, you have the files for the first semester now. I've unlocked the notes for the first five lectures. Work through them, and then complete the written assignments and send it over to me. Once I've had a look we'll arrange to meet again."

"Just like that," Hans grinned, a hint of a question in his voice.

Giles nodded his head once. "Just like that."

"Well, excellent. Thank you very much, sir. I'll go home and start working on it right now." He turned to go.

Giles had the impulse to ask where home was, but thought better of it. Didn't want to embarrass the boy. Or find out something he would regret knowing later. "Very good," he said, returning his gaze to his holo.

Hans started shuffling out of his office.

"Oh, and Hans?" Giles called after him.

"Yes, sir?"

"Don't make me regret this."

Hans nodded, "I promise you won't, sir. You can count on me."

"Yes," Giles agreed with more than a dose of skepticism. "I'm sure," he said, watching the boy wander out of his office.

Gaitune-67, Molly's Conference Room

Molly had just got up to her conference room from a quick few minutes of talking with Brock and Crash, who were back from vacation, when Giles stepped in and updated her regarding Hans.

She stared at him a moment, "So you've just decided to tutor him?" she asked.

Giles couldn't tell if Molly was mad at his rash decision or amused at his sentimentality.

"Well," Giles explained, "I made the offer to all three of them, but only Mr. Duo took me up on the offer."

Molly's expression relaxed and a definite smile spread across her lips. "Well I'll *be*," she breathed. "I never pegged you as someone who would take a charge under your wing..."

Giles took his glasses off and pinched his eyes. "I keep surprising even myself," he confessed.

"Quite," she agreed, raising one eyebrow. "So what did they tell you?"

Realizing this was going to be longer than a two second confession, Giles sat down on the opposite side of the conference table. Not so much so he was out of reach of a slap in case this went wrong, but more so he could watch Molly's reactions, in case she was inclined to give him a clue as to what she was really thinking.

"Well," he started with a deep breath, "it looks like we may have a political problem brewing."

Molly's eyes fixed attentively on him as she settled back in her seat.

Giles continued. "Said they were hired to, and I quote, 'disrupt the university and cause as much panic as possible.'"

He paused, scratching behind his ear, waiting for a reaction.

"And do we know who hired them?" she asked after a moment.

"Yes. Some guy called Arnold Sloth."

Molly shook her head. "Don't know him."

Giles bobbed his head and clasped his hands on the table in front on him. "He's a fixer. For some investment consortium on Ogg: the Northern Clan of Cambodian. They have some stake in maintaining the status quo of the Central Systems by the looks of their websites, but they don't disclose any details of the organizations they support."

Molly rubbed her chin and leaned forward, subconsciously mirroring his posture. "Interesting..." she agreed quietly.

"Anyway, we're still trying to figure out what the connection is, but thought you should be aware that someone out there is looking to make some moves against the university." He watched her carefully.

She reacted ever so slightly, her eyes narrowed with a hint of anxiety, despite her normally cool controlled exterior.

She was quiet, processing the information.

Or perhaps talking with Oz.

Or both.

"You're sure it's domestic?" she asked after a few moments.

Giles nodded and leaned back. "Pretty certain at this point. When you have armies at your control you don't hire college kids to rough people up."

"Of course."

Giles got up to leave.

Molly cocked her head, realizing something. "Hey Giles, when you said *we*... who did you mean exactly?"

Giles stopped dead in his tracks and backed up a couple of steps. "We?"

"Yeah. You said *we're* still trying to figure out..."

His face dropped. "Ah, yes," he said sheepishly, his heart rate increasing. "There is one more thing you ought to know..."

From outside the room there was an eerie silence for a moment. And then all that could be heard was an onslaught of bad language in Molly's screaming voice.

Paige and Maya's heads snapped to the direction of the conference room.

A grin spread mischievously across Paige's face. "That's more like the fireworks I was expecting the other day!"

196

Maya, by contrast, was horrified, and immediately did the only thing any sane person would do in such a situation. She hit her holo. "Oz. What's going on in there?"

"I probably shouldn't say," Oz replied through her audio implants.

Paige started chuckling to herself. "Oh, come on, Ozzy-baby. You can't keep all the gossip to yourself. Who's in there with her?"

"I'm sorry... I can't say."

Paige could detect the wavering in his ironically artificially generated voice.

She had him.

"Come on, Oz. You always want us to report in and keep you in the loop. Remember the girls' circle we let you in on so you could refine your heuristic algorithms. Relationships are two way streets, right?"

Maya's expression started to turn to one of amusement. "I can't believe you're using our girls' nights in to leverage an AI for intel!" she whispered to Paige. "Have you no morals?"

Paige's eyes danced with the twinkle of a thousand water-cooler moments to come. "Oz?" she pushed.

"Okay, okay," he relented, dropping his tone to a whisper in their implants. "You didn't hear it from me but it's Giles," he told them conspiratorially. "He's using students to investigate a criminal incident at the university."

Paige frowned. Then shrugged, exchanging glances with Maya. "Best way for them to learn, right?"

"That's what *he* said," Oz reported back.

Maya's lips were fixed in half a smile, not really knowing how to feel about the whole thing. "And Molly doesn't agree?" she asked.

"Duty of care seems to be her main argument at the moment."

There was a crash and a bang from the conference room.

The shouting stopped.

ELL LEIGH CLARKE & MICHAEL ANDERLE

Maya leaned closer to Paige, trying to see past the pillars around the common area through to the corridor. "I can't believe peer pressure worked!" Maya giggled again quietly to Paige.

Paige put one finger up. "They've stopped shouting." Her eyes were wide with concern. "Oz, what's happening."

"Erm… I'm not sure."

Paige pressed again. "Oz…" she repeated warningly.

Maya's eyes wrinkled in concern. Any humor she had been feeling was quickly evaporating. "Maybe we should go check on them?" she suggested.

"No. No," Oz told them both quickly. "You should definitely *not* go check on them."

The girls looked at each other, trying to fathom what might be going on. After all, Oz had direct access to what was going on through Molly's head. And… well, everything in her neurology.

He kept talking. "The best thing you can do is pretend you're not listening and head down to the basement. Hang out with Brock and Crash for half an hour."

Paige eyed the corridor suspiciously. "Why?"

"Trust me on this," Oz insisted.

Without another word, and feeling kind of stunned, Paige and Maya picked up their mochas and headed quickly over to the basement stairs.

Opening the door, they came across Joel. He was sweaty and still panting, wearing his workout gear with a towel slung over his shoulder.

"Hey!" Paige called brightly.

"Hey." Joel responded, a little taken aback by the forced brightness of Paige's greeting.

He looked over at Maya. She looked equally unnatural, like a elkinder caught in the headlights. "Hey," she parroted, awkwardly.

Joel smiled. "Well, er… good talking!" he muttered as he tried to side step them and make his way through the door.

Paige glanced at Maya and then back at Joel, her eyes suddenly wide. "How about you come back downstairs with us? We're just going to have a chat with Crash and Brock about their vacation."

Joel pointed up into the safe house. "I was just on the way to the kitchen."

"Ah, okay," Paige said. "What do you need?" she asked, handing her half cup of mocha to Maya. "I was just heading there myself."

Joel looked taken aback. "I was going to make a protein shake…" he said suspiciously.

Paige nodded as if taking mental notes. "Grass or fruit?"

"Fruit."

"Cinnamon?"

"Yes, please."

"Potato starch?"

"Yes, please."

"Juniper ginger?"

"Er, no. Thanks," he replied, falling in line with the conversation now as if talking with a barrister at a local Quazarbucks.

Paige nodded, accepting the order. "Okay. I'll grab it and be right down," she grinned, turned on her heels and glared pointedly at Maya to make sure she led him back down the stairs.

"But what's going on?" Joel protested as he allowed himself to be turned around by Maya and ushered into the basement.

Maya prodded him forward with her fingertips against his damp sweat suit, trying to avoid touching him as much as she possibly could. "Nothing. Nothing… just don't want you to miss this opportunity for team bonding," she cooed, finding her old journalistic improv game. "Remember what you taught us in drill training: the team is only as strong as its weakest link, and social bonding is of utmost importance."

The basement doors closed behind them, and Paige shook her head at the drama as she hurried to the kitchen. Busying herself, she carefully averted her ears from any sounds that may or may not have been going on in Molly's conference room. At this point, she realized, she just didn't want to know.

Gaitune-67, Safe house basement workshop

Joel and Maya arrived and found seats to join the conversation in the workshop.

Crash and Brock were all smiles and sun tans, sitting a little nervously in the new lounge area. Paige had taken the liberty of ordering up a few more sofas and comfy chairs while they had been away, and Sean had helped carry out the old broken one that they'd previously hijacked from under the theater stage.

Brock sat forward on one sofa, still acclimatizing to being back. "So, when are we going to meet him, Oz?"

Oz spoke through the holoscreen that had been there previously when they played video games. "Well, he's a bit busy at the moment."

"You MoFo! You have your kid working already?" Crash teased. "He's barely a few weeks old, and just arrived home... and you have him on assignment!"

The others laughed. Crash, sitting next to Brock, quietly chuckled to himself, his bouncing shoulders the only thing giving away that his was amused.

Sean was polishing his boots, which clearly didn't need that kind of treatment, but he had been insistent that old habits died hard, and that some were good for the soul while his mind seemed a galaxy away.

Oz's simulated expression appeared embarrassed. "Actually, he's binge watching the archives. He's discovered the Earth-style TV shows and, well... he won't spare any processing power to do anything else. I think he's hooked on something called *The Office*."

Maya caught the tail end of the conversation. "Well," she

exclaimed over Sean coming back to himself as he doubled over in laughter, "I hope he doesn't pick up any bad habits from that show. I've seen a few episodes. Not pretty in terms of human dynamics."

Oz's voice was serious. "I'll have a chat with him about the difference between television and reality."

"Said every parent under the Sark," chimed in Sean, "with zero effect!"

Maya smirked playfully. "Yeah, well, maybe have a chat with the Mollster, too. She's convinced there is such a thing as a time lord, and I swear she's waiting for him to swoop in and sweep her off her feet."

Paige arrived in time to hear Maya's statement. "Oh, she may well be over that delusion," she offered.

Joel frowned. "What makes you say that?"

"Oh nothing," Paige shrugged, handing Joel his protein shake. "Girl talk, is all. She's been talking about how she's resigning herself to what's right in front of her now."

Maya snickered. Brock eyed them with similar mirth as if he knew he'd be let in on whatever was going on. Sean and Joel shrugged, resigned to be outsiders on this particular circle of knowledge.

"So come on," Joel said, changing the subject, "enough about everything that's been happening here. How was the vacay?"

Brock's face lit up as he started telling stories, with Crash occasionally interjecting with details and qualifiers.

"Ohhh, my ancestors," Brock cried, "and what about that Dreifbýlistútta that would hang around the pool?"

Crash shook his head, shielding his eyes in shame. "The one who was always drunk..."

"Right!" Brock confirmed. Turning to the others he told them what had happened. "And each time I went down there and Crash was already there, I'd go down to find him hitting on Crash!"

ELL LEIGH CLARKE & MICHAEL ANDERLE

"Yeah," Crash interjected, almost as if his normally stoic persona was non-existent. "You just loved that. This guy," he said, jabbing Brock in the rib, "just sat at the bar and laughed, rather than stepping in to help me!" He looked to Sean for support.

Sean just grinned his rugged, amused grin.

The group continued their loud chatting and laughing.

"Well," Maya asked him over the ruckus, "what would you have had him do?"

Crash raised his hands in surrender. "I dunno. Maybe pretended to be my date? Or call me away for something important?"

Brock hid his face in his hands, laughing. "Dude, we weren't *working*. What kind of emergency could there have been?" He put on a fake emergency voice. "*Oh, Crash, I need you because we have a crisis with the mocha machine in our room!*"

More eruptions of laughter ensued from the group.

"Yeah," Brock said, "I don't think that would have worked."

Crash narrowed one eye at his friend and Brock patted him playfully on the leg. "There, there. You survived the big, mean, bar-drunk."

Maya and Paige chuckled, remembering their recent encounter in the bar.

Sean didn't look up, but kept polishing at his boots. "Well, it looks like you guys got more cozy, anyway."

Crash surprisingly didn't shut down. Brock grinned, leaving his hand on Crash's leg. "Well, maybe we did," he hinted, exchanging defiantly happy glances with Crash.

Paige clapped her hands together. "FINALLY!" she exclaimed excitedly. "I'm so happy for you guys!" She got up and hugged them. Maya did the same.

Joel, confused, watched the enthusiasm. Sean saw he was not catching on, again, but thought that it would do him more good to work it out for himself. Especially since he was supposed to be the people-savvy element of the leadership.

As the chatter continued the returned vacationers shared a few more tales of their adventures in Club Sark, at least until Sean happened to mention that he had nailed the level that neither he nor Crash could get past before they had gone away. This naturally led to the pair powering up the holosystem for Sean to demonstrate his video game prowess.

Brock turned his attentions to Paige. "So, how's the work going?"

Paige remained buoyant. "I need your help on the new range. We've got samples through, but I'm not sure they're going to hold up. The formula is different and we haven't battle tested it yet."

"Want me to give them a run?"

Paige grinned as if she'd been expecting him to jump to her aid. "Yes please! If you don't mind."

"Sure thing, girl. I gotcha." Paige had missed Brock's easy way and the way he just energized the space around him.

Paige and Brock continued their conversation, shifting closer together on the ends of their sofas and leaning in to have a more private conversation, and to be heard over the other conversations that had started.

"And how're sales going now?" Brock asked.

Paige pulled her lips to one side. "They've dropped off in the central systems a little, but our suppliers think it's just a seasonal issue. Ooooh!" she exclaimed suddenly, remembering something new. "Things are taking off in other systems though. Looks like we've got a preliminary meeting with DistriDen."

Brock's naturally supportive temperament exuded from his words. "Wow - that's amazing!"

"Yeah. It is. It's still early days - but looks like I might have to do a bit more traveling if it goes ahead."

Brock's voice dropped and he leaned in a little more. "What does that mean for your work here?"

Paige looked idly into her lukewarm mocha. "I dunno yet. I need to figure some things out and then of course talk to Molly."

"I see. I get it," he said bobbing his head. "Well, maybe we need to catch up properly later and you can tell me more about it over a couple of margaritas?"

Paige smiled weakly, knowing that it was something she was going to have to face. And she could think of no one better than Brock to help her figure it out. "Yeah, I'd like that." She turned and nudged Maya. "What do you think? Margarita Monday later?"

Maya nodded, grinning. "I'm in". She flashed her smile at Brock. She was glad he and Crash were back too. The place seemed incomplete without them.

Paige beamed like she used to before all the Carl business. "Good," she said firmly. "My room in two hours then!" She got up and trotted across to the stairs.

"Where you going?" Maya protested.

"That margarita mix isn't going to make itself!" she exclaimed, kicking her heel up with a little flair before skipping up the stairs to the safe house.

Maya shook her head giggling before moving over to Brock and Crash's sofa. She plonked herself in between them, her arms around them. "Have I mentioned that I'm soooooo glad you're both back?" she asked brightly.

Crash had been mid-game with Sean, but had the good sense to pause the game and give her a hug.

Brock squeezed her from the other side at the same time, and they both gave her a big smooch on either cheek.

Just then Jack wandered in. "Clearly I'm missing all the fun today," she remarked. Maya blushed and extracted herself from between her two friends and sat down on the other sofa again. Jack came to join her.

"So," Jack grinned, relaxing onto the sofa and plonking her feet on the mocha table. "How was the vacation?"

CHAPTER EIGHTEEN

Gaitune-67, Molly's Conference Room

Molly sat quietly in the conference room processing the evening's events. She felt good. But stunned.

I mean... Giles?

Her mind churned. Replaying the highlights.

Hey, wonder girl, I know you've got stuff going on, but we need to talk about Bourne.

Molly was non-responsive.

Molly!

She shook her head, forcibly pulling herself from her daydreams.

What?

It's Bourne. We need a plan.

What do you mean? He's safe now.

Yes, but what about his future? He's running through all the data we have access to, refining his algorithms as we speak. He'd maxing out all processing capabilities we've given him and constantly searching for me.

Of course he would. How much does he have compared to what you had at his age?

Probably about double right now.

Well, that's probably enough... for now. We don't know what affect those early years had on his core programming.

Oz suddenly remembered everything he went through with locking down his core and how hard some of those decisions were.

I'm going to need some help to guide him.

Well, I'm here. And we have ADAM too. He has lots of experience with this. Far more than we'll ever have.

Ok.

Oz?

Yes.

Are you... worried?

I'm concerned.

Which is just another word for worried.

Maybe.

Maybe is a deflection.

Ok. I'm worried. I'm concerned. I... I've never contemplated that this might happen. I'm making decisions at too high a rate, and I haven't got the bandwidth to figure out whether I'm making good decisions or not.

Molly smiled.

Are you mocking me?

No! Far from it. It's just you sound pretty much like a new human parent would sound.

Is that good?

It's not bad. It shows that you care. That you feel responsible for him. That you want the best for him.

I do.

Well then you're going to be a great parent.

I am?

Of course you are, Oz. What have you ever sucked at?

Oz vibrated in their shared neurology for a few moments.

Ah, well, nothing. You have a good point.

Well there we go. Nothing to worry about. And as things come up, we'll figure it out.

Just then the footsteps that had been clicking up the corridor stopped suddenly in a scuffle as Paige burst through the door. "Molly! I think we have a problem."

Paige was flushed from alcohol, and her make up was smudged.

Molly felt her stomach clench. "What's up?" she asked, concern descending on her like a sudden fog.

"Is Giles still here?"

Molly shook her head. "No, he left about ten minutes ago."

Paige stepped forward into the room. "Okay. We may need to get him back. He may have seen something."

Molly's mind whirred. "Seen what?"

Paige closed her eyes for a second to compose herself. "It's Sean. I went to find him to ask him about the Grincore System because… well. Anyway. He's not anywhere on the base. And then I asked Emma if he had left and she said no. But then she discovered that some of her records were out of sync and that something had been deleted."

Molly listened intently. She had a bad feeling about whatever was going on. Maybe her anxiety and befuddlement wasn't just because of her interlude with Giles. Maybe she had sensed something.

You can beat yourself up later, let's focus.

Molly turned her attention back on the intel coming at her.

"So he's left the base? And he's hiding that he's left?"

Paige nodded. "Yes. Then we discovered that the Scamp Princess was gone."

Molly felt her heart skip a beat. This was serious.

"Gone? Gone where?" Molly demanded, struggling to put words to her questions. "What does the tracking say?"

Paige's eyes were welling with tears. "Tracking has been disabled," she reported. "But I don't understand why he would.

Why wouldn't he tell us? Why would he hide where he was going?"

Just then Joel appeared in the doorway behind Paige. "What's going on?"

Paige repeated what she had just told Molly.

Joel's hand covered his mouth while he listened. When Paige was finished with the headlines, he removed his hand. "He's going on a mission," he posited. "Must be. And it must be on the DL."

Paige pulled up her holo. "Well then ADAM must know about it," she said, punching a message and asking Oz to contact him.

Moments later, Molly got the response via Oz. She shook her head. "Nope. He's not on anything for the Federation. ADAM hasn't heard from him. But Sean did receive an out of system message earlier today."

Paige frowned, her blue complexion getting grayer and grayer by the minute. "What does that mean?"

Joel's eyes darkened too, his concern growing. "Well, if it's not Federation business, it can only be personal."

Molly shifted on her chair and tapped the fingers on the table. "Which is why he's left us behind," she said, thinking out loud.

Joel looked at her in agreement. "Must be."

They mulled what was going on.

Paige broke them out of their thoughts. Her voice wavered with urgency now. "So what do we do?"

Molly stood up and said decisively, "Get ADAM to trace the origin of that call," she instructed Paige. "We're going after him."

Paige started to move but then hesitated. "But clearly he doesn't want us involved. What if it's personal?"

Molly shook her head. "Well then, he would have said that he needed some personal time. But he didn't. He took off. And did everything to cover his tracks. Which means he's in trouble of one kind or another, and he doesn't want to be followed."

Paige narrowed her eyes. "Which is why we're following him?"

Molly nodded. "Exactly. He's in trouble and probably thinks he can handle it himself. But friends don't let friends deal with their hardest challenges alone. We're going after him."

Paige didn't need any more explanation. She flew off down the corridor, very quickly sobering up.

Arlene's lab, Level 2, Skóli Uppstigs Academy

Giles shifted awkwardly against the table he was perched on. It was late in the evening but Arlene was still working. She called it her solace and Giles knew she often used her work as a form of meditation. He wasn't surprised to have caught her here. And with everything going on, it was about time he followed up with her about Anne.

Besides, it was a welcome, and tangible, distraction from the emotions he was close to being overwhelmed by.

"So you'll meet her?" he asked.

Arlene threw her arms up as she spun around to look at him. "You dangle a key to everything we've been working on for the last seven decades and you think I have a choice?" She was exasperated, but he could see the excitement in her eyes. "Of course I'll meet her," she huffed playfully.

Giles smiled inwardly, though his expression was still serious. "You realize she'll need your help?"

"Yes, I understand that." Arlene perched against her work bench and regarded him carefully. "I mean, when do they not?"

Giles was ready to defend himself… until she allowed a smile to escape.

"You're pulling my leg?" he realized.

She nodded, turning back to her holo. "A little."

Giles scratched his head. For him, working with women was a cross between herding sphinx and trying to comprehend the mating rituals of lanabeasts. Both of which were skills he sadly lacked.

"When do you want to meet her?" he asked cautiously, as if he may be being led into a trap.

Arlene shrugged and started tidying up pieces of lab equipment that had been left on the workbench. "Whenever," she said simply. "Although, you've got to promise this is a joint effort. You're not going to just ditch me with your charge and then leave me to do all the mentoring and training."

Giles started to protest, his expression a mixture of indignation and innocence around the accusation. "I..."

Arlene reeled around and pointed her finger at him. "Say it, space boy. She's *your* responsibility and I'm just helping you with her."

Giles threw his hands up in surrender. "Yes, yes. I agree."

Arlene carried on tidying the lab equipment up. Giles added more quietly, "We're in this together."

Arlene didn't react and Giles didn't push it.

Arlene started muttering away quietly. "It's like you give me a child to look after and then swam off without any recourse. I don't want to have to raise another one, which is what this will be," she added. "You hear me?" she said more loudly.

"Yes, I hear you," he confirmed obediently, folding his arms and settling himself down.

Arlene still had her back to him as she worked away. "Anything else you'd like to tell me?" she asked. "You seem... different."

Giles felt his heart rate increase. "How so?" he asked, as innocently as he could muster.

"Like you're hiding something," she told him.

"What could I possibly be hiding?"

"I dunno. But it's like you have a spring in your step. Which isn't like you... unless...?"

Arlene stopped, turned around and regarded him suspiciously.

"What?" he asked defensively.

"Unless..." she said slowly, unknowingly keeping him in suspense, "you've got a new project?"

Giles tried not to allow his exhale of relief be obvious. "Nope. No new project. Unless, of course, you count dear little Anne. And I can assure you mentoring isn't the kind of project that puts a spring in my step."

"Unconvinced," Arlene proclaimed, waving a hand. "After all, I heard about your other little mentoring project."

Giles looked confused.

"The smoke bomb guy," she clarified, turning around after moving a book.

"Oh yes," he said, relieved. "Well... one less ignorant mind on the planet..." he tried to justify.

Arlene chuckled to herself, turning to look at him again. "You don't fool me, Professor Kurns."

Giles regained his game. "I wasn't trying to."

Arlene's chuckling subsided. "Look, I know you love it really. Teaching. Educating. We've landed in your dream day job!" she exclaimed with a graceful wave of her arms, as if bowing to the room. "If space anthropology field work were ever off the table..."

Giles smiled awkwardly as he took off his glasses to clean them. "Well, yes," he conceded. "I expect you're right."

"*Meanwhile*," she noted a little more pointedly, "one of us has to do some real work... else we'll be stuck here forever." She turned her attention back to organizing some samples on the bench next to her.

"Yes, how's it coming?" he asked, glad for the change of subject.

She shook her head. "Slooooowly."

"Where are we at?"

"Well," she sighed, pulling a tray from a drawer off to her right. She plonked it down on the table where Giles was perched. "It seems that there is DNA in it. Hence the…" she gestured at the microscope and the samples scattered everywhere.

Giles looked intrigued as he hurriedly put his glasses back on - as if they actually did anything for him being able to see better. "You mean of a species?"

Arlene pursed her lips. "No. Can't seem to get it to match anything resembling life. Too chaotic."

Giles frowned, looking from the talisman to his partner in crime. "You think it might be just a data storage thing?"

Arlene raised her eyebrows. "Possibly," she agreed optimistically. "I'm working at trying to decode it. It's just taking forever."

Giles poked at the talisman, remembering the saga they had been through to acquire it. "Anything you can give ADAM to process?" he mused, almost to himself, as his creative mind churned.

"Not yet," she said, her lips firmly together in concentration. "Not until I've got a handle on a few creative leaps to try on him."

Giles nodded, his eyes still on the talisman. "Okay. Anything I can do?" he mumbled half heartedly.

"Yes!" Arlene told him sharply. "Stop bringing me little girls with energy problems!"

"Sorry," he replied spontaneously. He paused, catching up to her comment. "I'll do my best."

Arlene picked up the tray and placed it back in the draw and then shuffled between the drawer and her microscope, tidying up samples. "Yeah, between you with Anne, and now Molly's problem, it'll be a miracle if I get any work done at all."

Giles froze. "Molly has a problem?"

"Hmmm, I'm not entirely sure yet," she replied, oblivious to Giles's guilty expression. "Sean was going to talk to me again when he gets a minute."

"Anything serious?" he asked as casually as he could manage.

"I dunno," she shrugged. "She's walking a path very few have ever been through in one life time. We'll have to see."

Giles contemplated asking more, but then figured anything else could look suspicious. *Damn*, he wished he knew where he stood with Molly now. It would make everything so much easier.

Arlene returned to busying herself with work. He saw an escape and started heading towards the door. "Okay," he called back to her as he walked. "I'll bring Anne by soon then!"

"Okay, fine," Arlene agreed, her voice muffled by the microscope she was once again peering down. "And in the meantime I'll try not to die from mundanity!" she added as his footsteps disappeared into the corridor beyond.

CHAPTER NINETEEN

Aboard the Scamp Princess, unknown location

"Sean?"

"Yes, Scamp."

"Those coordinates we're heading towards…"

"Yes?"

"My sensors are telling me that there's nothing there."

"Yes. That's right." Sean closed the holo video he'd been rewatching for the hundredth time and swiveled round to check the instruments and readings that Scamp was talking about.

"So why are we going there?" Scamp asked, confused.

"Because that's where we need to be to receive the coordinates of where we're actually going."

Scamp's simulated voice cracked over the aging intercom. "How does that work?"

Sean wasn't making this discussion EI-friendly at all.

"Well, this is where my friend — and I use the term loosely — and I decided would be our transmission point. If we ever needed to meet again."

"How do you mean?" Scamp appeared as a visual simulation

on the console in front of Sean, as if giving Sean a focal point might actually help in extracting an explanation from him.

"Well," Sean started slowly, "a long time ago while you were still in the employ of our illustrious Empress... I met a girl."

Scamp's expression changed to one of genuine surprise. "Oh. You were involved?"

"Yes, you could say that. But things happened and she was in trouble. I helped her out and things... *happened*."

Scamp raised one simulated eyebrow. "You're being very vague. I hope you're not this amorphous on your mission reports. It could make for some very unsatisfying reading."

Sean's face suddenly looked old. "Well..." he sighed. "Long story short, we had to part company to make sure we were both going to be safe. And because... well, I couldn't guarantee I wasn't going to kill her myself, between her annoying habits and bone-headedness."

Scamp chuckled over the intercom. It sounded like a combination of kittens giggling crossed with claws down a blackboard. "Sounds like a match made in heaven," she teased.

Sean scowled. "Not even a little bit. Anyway, this was the pick up point where if we needed to be in touch with one another, we would send a message to a special server, and then transmit the meeting point coordinates to this spot."

Scamp frowned, still befuddled by this strange protocol. "Why wouldn't you just send them in the initial message?"

"Because," Sean explained, "if the message were ever intercepted then our meeting would be compromised."

There was a pause, then Scamp confirmed. "I understand."

"Cool," Sean acknowledged, going back to monitoring his instruments. "And just keep that to yourself, eh? I don't want Molly and the others finding out."

"Why not?"

"Because I don't want them following me, or getting involved in anything in the future," he said, a hint of frustration in his voice. "The less they know the better."

Scamp once again displayed his preset "confused face." "But I'm sure if they knew your problem they would be more than happy to help. Molly helped Joel with one of his things a few weeks ago."

Sean looked up, "What thing?"

"Oh. You didn't know?" Scamp cooed coolly. "I guess this is what happens when people keep secrets." She looked satisfied that she had made his point cleverly.

"Look Scamp, I'm not keeping secrets for the sake of being mysterious," Sean retorted. "I'm trying to keep my friends safe. Yes, Molly would be behind me on this in an instant, but I'd never forgive myself if anything happened to any of them as a result of something I dragged them into."

Scamp shook his virtual head. "I'm sure they wouldn't agree with that."

"Maybe not," Sean agreed, "but this is *my* mess, and I'm taking care of it. If they know anything, they'd be at risk. If they came with me, they'd be at risk. And quite honestly, I don't even know if I'm coming back from this alive."

Scamp's representation on screen morphed into an expression of concern. "How do you mean?"

"This friend…" Sean confessed, "she was mixed up with some very dangerous people. That's all you need to know." His tone was definite.

Scamp had the sophistication to recognize the vocal nuance. "Okay, Sean. I'll respect that. For *now*. But if there is anything that pertains to this operation you need to start talking before we get to that meeting point. I need to be fully briefed."

Sean sighed and sat back in the console chair. Scamp was right. And if Scamp was going to go along with his secrecy thing, then he owed her the full story.

Just then the message screen started flashing, and Sean sat up.

"Looks like your coordinates just came in," Scamp reported.

"Great!" he said, a little more engaged now that there was progress. "Set a course," he instructed. "And then I'll tell you everything you need to know for the next phase of our little escapade."

The ship hovered in mid-space light years from anything for a few seconds. And then it vanished, leaving only the trace of a gate jump.

Sean Royale truly was on his own now.

"So." Sean laid his head back on the seats headrest. "There was a girl."

"This sounds like the typical start of a bad situation," Scamp interjected.

Sean looked over at Scamp's face on the screen. "That's because it is, and who is telling this story?"

"Well, you. However, you aren't doing it very quickly," Scamp replied.

"That's because stories that start 'there was a girl' usually hurt and it takes a bit to be willing to yank that bandage off."

"Oh."

"So," Sean started again. "There was a girl…"

This time, Scamp didn't interrupt.

EPILOGUE

Common area, Gaitune-67

Oz's voice interrupted the chattering in their audio implants. "Hey, I'm here."

Paige and Maya looked at each other, then glanced around conspiratorially.

"Ok, go ahead," Paige whispered taking a sip of her sneaky home-made margarita.

They'd been working for 48 hours straight since they found out about Sean, and even though they were intent on running down every dead end lead they could come up with Molly and Joel had insisted they take a break, have a drink and then get some rack time.

"I brought Bourne," Oz explained. "I figured you two are safe… as in, not going to fill his fragile little mind with death and destruction."

Paige raised one eyebrow, more for Maya's benefit than anything. "Who says? If you don't spill on what you know, there may be carnage… of the cyber variety!"

Oz chuckled. "Well, we'll see. But remember my loyalty is to Molly first."

Another voice interrupted on their implants. "I don't know why I even need to be here. I was perfectly hap-"

Oz interrupted the second voice. "Bourne, binge-watching Netflix is not the same as getting real-life interactions."

Bourne's digitally rough voice responded. "It is. I'm even learning about vampires."

Maya's lips turned up into a half-smile. "What's he watching?" she asked with morbid curiosity.

"Vampire Diaries," Oz responded. Maya could almost hear the eyeroll in his voice.

Paige sniggered. "LOVE that show…"

"Besides," Oz continued parenting Bourne, "you do realize that the representation they have of vampires is completely off kilter with real life, right?"

Bourne muttered something which Paige and Maya couldn't make out.

"Wow…" Paige commented, "teenage years come quick when you're an AI, eh?"

Oz sighed. "You're frikkin' telling me…"

Maya suddenly thought of something, almost spilling her drink. "Ooo – before I forget," she said. "I was made on the mili-tary-base, right? They would have had me on video walking in and out of there?"

Paige's eyes flickered in recognition. In amongst everything she'd forgotten that detail.

"Yes," Oz confirmed. "Although I've already enacted the same online protocol I've been using for Molly."

Maya frowned. "What's that?"

Oz loved these moments. "Well, since there is no way I can stop you people from walking around and drawing attention to yourselves, I realized I needed to make sure that every image of you that is ever put online needs to be… corrupted… in some way to avoid being flagged as a match by facial recognition."

Maya was tech-savvy. And yet she was still frowning in confusion. "What does that *mean?*"

Oz had a smile in his tone. "Quite simply I just make sure that the faces and various features like height and build are... *altered...* so that the systems can't detect them as a match."

Paige looked horrified for a moment. "You're not altering us to make us look ugly are you?"

Oz was audibly chuckling now. "Well, ugly is such a subjective term. But no. I don't think so. Just changing the proportions enough so as to throw the algorithms. That's all."

Paige looked somewhat relieved. "But why don't you just take them down?"

"And draw even more attention?" Oz chuffed. "Yeah, I was doing that, but then the disappearance of the images was making things more complicated. And then Molly went and started the university and... well, let's just say that Estarians have their comfort levels and having a board member whose image kept disappearing was spooking them."

Maya giggled and covered her mouth with her hand.

"Well, ok then," she said, evidently convinced she wasn't going to have the military on her tail. "Now onto the important questions. We're dying to know... what the hell was going on with Molly and Giles? It was Giles in there with her the other day right?"

Their audio implants were quiet for a moment while Oz processed what he was going to say. "Ok," he said finally. "Yes. It *was* Giles. And yes, something *did* happ-"

"I *KNEW* it!" Maya exclaimed, suddenly animated, snapping her fingers. Excitement vibrated through her whole persona. "And good on her. About time one of these dudes stepped up and..." She stopped, realizing she was about to be crude.

About their boss.

And their friend.

Then she noticed Paige's expression: it was one of immediate concern layered on top of the existing anxiety of their missing team mate and friend.

"What is it?" Maya asked.

Paige tipped her head slowly to one side, searching to put words to her feelings. "I dunno. I mean, I didn't like Giles at first. But he's kinda grown on me... especially since he stepped up into this being all he can be and tackling the talisman quest and all..."

"And his role at the university... to support Molly," Maya interjected.

"Yes... and yet. I dunno." Paige's shoulders dropped an inch. "I just feel like it's a bit..."

She didn't finish the thought.

"Sudden?" Maya offered.

"Reactionary," Paige decided. "I mean, she just reconnected with her parents, she's got tons going on with the university and some unknown threat. She has the responsibility of a new baby."

"I'm hardly a baby," Bourne interjected.

Paige continued, ignoring Bourne's comment. "... and then I'm sure there's something else going on with her. Something realm related...but she just hasn't had chance to deal with it all."

Maya was bobbing her head gently. "So you're thinking that her thing with Giles is just a reaction?"

"Maybe." Paige confessed.

"Well, good for her," Maya concluded. "I mean, we cope how we cope," she added, raising her margarita glass.

Paige remained unconvinced. "I suppose," she said, taking a sip of her own drink.

Oz piped up. "If I may..." he said, inserting himself into the analysis. "I think Paige is right. Molly has a lot going on, and as her friends who love her very much, we're right to be concerned. The other thing that we have to remember is that that she is a grown-ass adult, more than capable of making her own decisions. And whatever we think of Giles, or the Molly and Giles combo, we have to respect Molly's choices."

"And be there to pick up the pieces when it all goes to shit?" Paige muttered sullenly from over her margarita glass.

"M-iles!" Bourne added, chuckling to himself.

Maya ignored the other two's comments. "Looks like someone was binge watching Dr. Phil, Oz-man!"

Oz was confused. "How did you know?" he asked, not understanding the connection.

Maya popped her glass down and wiped a sticky finger on her napkin. "You're starting to sound like a tv talk show host!" she explained.

Bourne saw his chance to derail the conversation. "I don't understand, Oz. You're like me. You don't have feelings. How can you say you *love* Molly?"

If Oz had a face, Paige imagined he would have been smiling sagely. "I do. She's my person. And it's difficult to explain until you've had someone like that in your life… But come, we'll talk about that and let the girls get some rest. After all, they *are* under orders."

"Alright, Pops. But then I'm going back to Vampire Diaries. I'm right at the bit wher-"

"Lalalalalalala," Paige started singing.

"What's up with her?" Bourne asked.

Maya chuckled. "She's only seen up to the end of season six and doesn't want to hear any spoilers!"

"Oh my," Bourne exclaimed in an accent and tone he was clearly mimicking from something he'd seen. "I didn't realize you people still watched these arcane files."

Maya grinned knowingly. "Oh, it's a guilty pleasure of a number of people on this base," she revealed. "Even people you probably wouldn't suspect!"

"Anyway, I'll leave you with this," Oz continued, returning the conversation to his last point. "We may or may not agree with Molly's choice here, but we should at least trust her. And if she is processing stuff, then… well, maybe this is part of it. And if it turns out that she and Giles make a go of it, well we should be happy for them."

Paige pulled a face, the alcohol clearly kicking in and lowering her normal inhibitions. Maya nudged her and pulled a goofy face to pull her out of her downer.

"Ok," Oz said, wrapping up, "I've got parenting to do. And I need to figure out how to explain different types of love to baby Bourne..."

"I'm NOT a BABY!" Bourne argued over the connection.

Paige could have sworn she heard Oz sigh.

"Ok, later ladies," Oz added.

And then they were gone.

Maya and Paige looked at each other again, processing the conversation.

"So?" Maya ventured.

Paige took a deep breath, as if to impart some newly realized wisdom.

"I need another drink," she concluded, and shuffled off the sofa to grab the rest of the mix from the kitchen.

FINIS

HOLO TRANSMISSION FROM OZ

Greetings of the day upon you.

Oz here.

Molly has asked me to be the liaison between her operation and your rather primitive earth communication methods.

I believe you call it *email?*

Still.

I am here to act as your interface. To help bridge the gap between the dopamine induced hits as you watch Molly through her trials and tribulations as she takes on all manner of shenanigans.

If you'd like to receive such status updates, please go ahead and leave your holo/ email address here:

http://ellleighclarke.com/

As you might have gathered, this transmission will not just be coming through space between our two galaxies, but is also traveling back through time.

I will attempt to send you updates in chronological order but do be advised that occasionally gravitational optics will interfere (no pun intended!) with the sequencing of these packets.

An understanding of all things timey-whimey will be useful in such instances.

Additionally, if you have any feedback for Molly - or her team - do feel free to pass that on through me. All you need to do is hit reply to any of my messages.

I process every communication personally.

Looking forward to hearing from you.

Oz

(on behalf of Molly, *aka the lady- boss*)

Sanguine Squadron 2.0

Gaitune-67,

Sark System,

Loop Galaxy

AUTHOR NOTES - ELL LEIGH CLARKE
JANUARY 7, 2018

Thank yous

As always I'd like to thank MA for his continued support in navigating the publishing jungle. Thanks is also due for him stepping up during my trans-America relocation and taking on the final punch of this manuscript. It was a huge help and meant that we could get this into reader hands weeks faster that it would otherwise have taken me on my own.

In the same vein I'd like to send a massive gratitude bomb out to members of the beta reader team who over Christmas peeled themselves away from turkey duties and family to skim sections of the books to fact check so that I could keep writing. Robert, Joshua, Charles, Ron... You're the best. I'm so grateful to you and appreciate you volunteering to help so quickly. It was like a dream come true having the answers that were holding me back just handed to me on platter. Or in a slack channel, as it turned out to be. Thank you!

I'd also like to thank Trausti Trauterson, my cool Icelandic friend for helping name the university. For those who aren't fluent in Icelandic, *Skóli Uppstigs Academy* means *Ascension Academy*. As you probably know if you've been reading these notes from the beginning, Trausti also helps with the supply of creative Icelandic (Estarian) swearing.

He also reliably informed me that the word we used: Dreif-býlistútta, means something like hill billy/ tit/ or boob.

Cracks. Me. Up!

Massive thanks also goes out to Steve Campbell and his incredible team of JITers for wrangling this manuscript so quickly, and catching typos and inconsistencies. You're the best!

I'd also like to thank the ever-patient Joe Brewer for his expert editing and fixing my messes(!) with zero fuss and drama. Joe, you're a gem. Thank you for everything you do.

And finally I'd like to thank YOU – the reader - not just for buying and reading this book, but for leaving your awesome (and often amusing!) 5* reviews. I massively appreciate your kind words both on Amazon and on our facebook page. You so often keep me going. I know you've been forced to wait waaaay too long for this latest instalment and I deeply appreciate not just your patience, but your compassionate support as I've been working through stuff. Thank you. Thank you. Thank you. <3

A way too honest account

I finished listing off the cocktails of drugs I'd been taking.

Dr. Awesome, also known to some of us as Dr. HOTsome, leaned forward on the desk and put his head in his hands.

"I don't take them all, all the time," I explained.

He looked up with almost a glimmer of hope.

"Ok," I qualified. "So I take *most* of them, *a lot* of the time."

His head went back into his hands.

This was the man who had pulled me back from the brink of total health collapse only months previously. My body had decided it was done writing at the rate of a sprint with the distance of a marathon. It had taken weeks and weeks, and all kinds of medical badassery, but it worked. I had been functioning again.

In fact, I had even been optimistic about the future. I'd been starting to think about expanding into my own series, starting a software company and getting back to a bunch of other projects I'd been spinning before I crashed.

But that was before.

Now, following a couple of traumatizing situations, I sat before him a broken shell, teetering on the brink of drug addiction to cope.

More than once in the weeks prior I'd been drifting off to sleep having taken fuck-knows what, scared that I wasn't going to wake up the next morning. I feared my mother getting a call from some random police officer who had managed to track down my next of kin weeks after my death to notify her that her daughter would never be coming home from this dangerous land.

Granted I was somewhat stabilized since our previous meeting when I'd been bouncing along rock bottom.

But I was barely keeping it together.

"The painkillers help me sleep," I told him, trying to show there was some logic to what I was doing. "Coz the only reason I'm not sleeping is because it hurts so much."

He lifted his head from his hands once again and looked at me curiously. "What hurts?"

"My heart."

"Tell me more about that," he said. He already knew what had happened a few months before. He'd figured it out. I didn't need to tell him the story. Now, he just wanted to know about the symptom.

"Like chest pain," I said, trying to explain that it was physical.

"In your heart?"

I nodded.

"Stand up..." He came over and started pressing on my back where one might stab a knife if one was so inclined. "Does that hurt?" he asked prodding gently.

I shook my head.

"What about that?"

I winced. "Yes."

"That?"

"Yes."

I was nervous. I don't do too well with people being close to me. It wasn't that he wasn't safe to be around. Far from it. He's one of the few people I'd like to be around more. But while he was working on my heart, I didn't dare tell him it wasn't quite in my chest anymore.

It was in my throat. (Why? What were you thinking? Where did you think it was gonna be?!)

Breathe Ellie, I told myself, hiding under my oversized cardigan.

"Ok," he said, "I'm going to adjust you."

He stepped closer, explaining the action, and a flood of emotions ran through me. I froze, trying to engage my brain while dealing with all these feelings.

"Put your arms up, do this, then interlock your fingers on top of mine," he told me standing behind me.

Ok, so this isn't sounding like a consultation in a doctor's office, but it was nothing but appropriate and professional.

At least on his side.

I was a mass of emotions, vulnerability and a whole heap of other stuff I'm not going to admit to here.

What followed was a kinda James Bond maneuver - except I don't believe he was trying to kill me.

My ribs on my back cracked.

Emotion released.

It felt strangely better.

Ok good. Now I get to hug the doctor and then we go back to talking from a safe distance where he can't hear my heart beating in my throat.

Or not.

"Lie on your nose," he instructed pointing at the couch.

I hesitated processing what I needed to do. I looked at the

couch. My mind spun. Do I take my shoes off? The paper is going to slip... my mind raced to process meaningless information.

I got onto the couch and planted my nose into the tissue. It smelled of chocolate. It was actually a small relief to hide my face and ignore the ridiculous stream of emotions that were running through my system.

He started poking around the area on my back where my heart would be. It was the same - pain all around the heart.

Fine everywhere else.

"Breathe in and then exhale," he told me.

And with that his hand gently pushed the ribs in just the right place to elicit a crack, releasing another tonne of emotion.

"Fuck!" I breathed from under his hand.

It was a good 'fuck'.

And a *surprised* 'fuck'.

And it only hurt a little bit.

He rubbed the area dissipating the energy. It felt a little better. Like a relief, that the body hadn't quite caught up to understanding yet.

I got up, and the rest is a blur, until he told me to lie down again, this time on my head.

I figured that meant on my back.

He started inspecting the front of my chest around my heart.

"Say when it hurts," he told me.

He poked gently around my rib cage. "Here?"

"No that's ok."

"This?"

"No."

"This?"

"YES!"

FUUUUUUUuuucccccck, I screamed in my head.

His finger stayed. Searing pain like a hot knife sliced through the pericardium.

I should have left it there but I panicked and burst into tears, lifting his hands firmly from my ribs and away from the wound.

Agony that I'd been suffering with for the last two months exploded through my chest, releasing in physical hurt and emotion.

I wanted to run. I didn't want him to see me like this.

And at the same time I knew I was in exactly where I needed to be.

When it all subsided, I was a mess of tears and mascara. And Doctor Awesome was there, being... well, Awesome.

What I didn't realise at the time was that this moment changed EVERYTHING.

--

The next day I felt like a different person.

My heart didn't feel as sore.

I realized that that night I'd fallen asleep at a reasonable hour, rather than spending the time until first light writhing with hurt that the drugs would barely touch. It was a weird, but very welcome, sensation.

I rolled over to check my phone.

Mum had messaged.

My Nanna had passed away.

We'd been expecting it so it wasn't a shock. I'd been dreading it happening though - even though I knew I'd see her again soon. (Yeah, I maybe I need a shrink too - but yes I see people who have crossed over. A lot. In fact, I'm closer to my Gran now more than when she was alive.)

But the whole death thing can bring up all kinds of grief and before that morning I honestly didn't think my heart would be able to take it. Literally. I figured the chakra was collapsed and that was it until something changed.

And yet, that morning, I was ok.

I tuned in to see if I could see Nanna... but she wasn't around yet.

I got on with my day: did some consulting calls, a mastermind online group call, and called my Mum.

And I was ok.

Ok, so the discomfort wasn't *completely* gone. But it felt more like an injury that was healing than an open hemorrhaging gash of despair and excruciating pain.

I could barely hope it was real, but I kept reminding myself that it totally could be healing.

I mailed the good doctor. He suggested I write up my author notes today - possibly while things were going good ...and I wasn't still resentful about him taking me off coffee!

So this is the account you're reading right now.

P.S. It's evening time now on as I'm writing this, and I just smelled Nanna's moisturizer in my hand cream. She used to use Oil of Olay. She'd call it Oil of Ugly. Bless her. She was anything but ugly. I hope she likes her new place. I wonder if she's found Granddad yet... <3

P.P.S. I'm editing this for punctuation a day later and am happy to report in that Nanna popped in to let me know that she had found Granddad and all was well. :)

Since then things have been on the up and up. Ok, so there was one debilitating relapse which took me out for 48 hours, but generally I think I'm on the mend.

I've barely needed any drugs so I've not been worrying about overdosing or wrecking my liver just trying to get through the night. Granted, one never knows when one's time is up, but for the most part my immediate concern about my Mum getting that dreadful phone call is gone.

This really was a turning point.

Dr. Awesome, if you're reading this, from the bottom of my (broken!) heart: thank you for saving my life.

And for being, well,... *Awesome*.
Here's to the next chapter.

Parties, Wine and Mojo
I have a party trick.
While some people have tricks they do with pennies and beer, or shot glasses and beer mats, mine is a little more... out there.
I change the taste of wine.
By charging it with energy.
From my hands.
Yup. You read that right.
Now bear with me before you start phoning round to see if you can get me committed. I know this is a little off the wall, but by the time you've finished reading these notes you'll know how to do it yourself.
(And that will *really* mess with your head if you're not already down with the woo!)
I showed it to Steve Campbell and his friend Bob when we were in Vegas for the 50Books conference.
Bob is a wine connoisseur. I figured that if there was any change in the wine, then Bob would be able to taste the difference.
Now, as you know I've been subpar for about a year now and I didn't know if it would work.
So, putting all attachment and ego aside, I set up an experiment anyway. Two glasses of wine: one the test, one the control. (As you know wine oxidizes once it's been exposed to air, so the taste will naturally evolve over time. Hence the extra need for the control. You wanna know that the change in the taste is due only to the variable and not the oxidation.)
Next you hold your hand over the glass, and then in the same way that Arlene will conjure a fire ball, you just focus your inten-

tion into the glass from your hand, drawing energy through your higher chakras so you don't deplete your own reserves. (Your cells need it to live!)

And whereas Arlene would *throw* a fireball, you're dealing with a glass a wine. You don't need to go kung fu on its ass. You just want to kinda pour the energy in. Gently!

Regarding the intention to use, I use things like "gratitude", or "love". Then all you do is hold the feeling in your body and then project it into the molecular structure of the liquid*.

Anyway, there I was sitting with Bob and Steve, knowing I couldn't even feel my own energy, but trying this thing anyway.

And long story short, it worked.

Yay!

Bob was adequately freaked out, and then resigned himself to not being able to explain it. Then the dinner continued.

But here's the problem that crept into my awareness. It took several goes and many minutes of sitting there with my hand over the glass (like a muppet, I might add). Plus, when I put my hands together I couldn't feel the force that would normally come through them.

I must say, I didn't think much of it again.

That was until I was at that doctor's appointment and I felt the kick back from Dr. Awesome's energy field.

When he left me alone in the office to organize some treatments I remembered Vegas. I remembered how I had struggled to work my mojo on the wine, and the lack of energy in my hands.

In the quietness I put my hands together.

Still nothing.

It was like my heart had collapsed and the energy was no longer flowing, similar to if an engine had just stopped.

But I could feel Dr. Awesome's as he reiki'd me, as strongly as if someone were touching my skin... and deeper.

Something was wrong with me.

I filed it in my head to revisit later. Later as in when my heart wasn't crippling me and I had some energy back.

So fast forward several days, and sitting in my hotel room in LA before heading to Austin, knowing that the manuscript and cover were being worked on and everything squared away for the move, my thoughts returned to the energy conundrum.

I'd been feeling better since the heart healing with Dr. A - bar a brief relapse which I eventually crawled back from.

So I put my hands close together to see if I could tune in and maybe even get it working again...

And lo and behold, it was back!

Y-frikkin-AYYYYYYYY!

I could feel my energy field again!!!

Ok, so it was about as strong as when you have those little magnets at school and you put two like-poles together.

But it was start.

And it gave me something to build on.

I'm sure there's more for me to work through, and this isn't the end of the story, but I really feel like this is a turning point in everything.

And I can't wait for what comes next.

Footnote. *(I'm assuming we can do footnotes within author notes... yeah? It feels kinda like a footnote to a footnote!) Shit, suddenly I'm feeling like an academic again.*

Ok, here's the other side of that little ol' asterisk which you probably skipped passed earlier on when I was describing the process of charging the wine with an intention. --->>>

*You can do it with food, pet's, objects, people... anything really.

Eventually you can do it without your hand, and just project your energy around it.

I started doing it when I saw the Emoto studies of water crystals that proved that human intentions change the crystalline structure of the water. It all just seemed to make sense.

I get a kick out of the stunned looks as scientists, medics and people with no belief in the unseen taste the sample glass, and the control glass - and then have to admit that there is a difference.

I get an **even bigger** kick when someone does it for themselves.

And this is the thing: with practice, anyone can do it.

ANYONE.

(Heck I *just* about managed it when I was broken as all fuck.)

I've seen folks pick it up over breakfast at my masterminds. I've seen people do it at a dinner party or in a restaurant.

All you need to an open mind and the ability to focus.

And that's it.

I'd love to know if you give it a go and get a result! Hit me up on the fb page and tell me about it, yeah? www.facebook.com/ellleighclarke.

I can't wait to see what you do!

Ellie x

AUTHOR NOTES - MICHAEL ANDERLE
JANUARY 7, 2018

Thank You's

First, thank YOU for not only reading this story about Molly, but also reading through our author notes here at the end!

Second, I'm going to thank Ellie for being a wonderful person who cares about people, and tries damned hard to be right with the universe, when the universe doesn't seem to try at all to be right with her.

And by doing so, she points out how we (or at least I) can take away just a smidgeon of her strength and apply some of her beliefs (or party tricks, or magic – whatever you are comfortable calling it) into my own life.

Hopefully, I don't set anything on fire.

I've mentioned before that I suspect Ellie is the next generation of Isaac Asimov, except she has a better accent. But, that could just by my Americanism showing.

Don't Fuck Up.

So, I'm coming into the new year, and I can't seem to get my head screwed back on properly. I'm talking with Ellie, realizing she is still in California when I thought she was hanging out in Texas, waiting for her furniture to arrive.

It seems that her furniture won't arrive for a couple of weeks and she has a 'plan.'

Except, this plan includes the store IKEA, and she has shared before how her and IKEA work.

It goes something like this:

1. 1)Ellie goes to IKEA (or shops online, I really don't know which) and orders / purchases one of their products.
2. 2)Said product arrives and sits on the floor and waits for Ellie to put it together.
3. 3)Product decides to mope, as it is receiving *NO* attention from Ellie.
4. 4)Product finally gets attention and is put together some weeks or months after purchase.

So, I ask how is this going to work with her purchasing IKEA, and needing a bed? She explains she has purchased a couch she can sleep on, and said couch hopefully only comes in a couple of pieces.

I sure hope so, or she will be sleeping on an IKEA box, I think. Or, there is a shitake ton of handy guys in Texas that would put her furniture together for a six-pack of Shiner.

Hell, maybe just so she would talk with them. Maybe that's a thing on Twitter she can search?

#WillPutIKEAFurnitureTogetherToHearBritishAccent.

I don't do Twitter, but I doubt it would be a good way to find a handy guy.

Now, after this conversation above she mentions the challenges (or did this happen first?) with her latest book, and what she is doing.

She has completed four chapters, and has the rest to go, needs to leave her apartment, get a room at the hotel, leave the next day, deal with covers and ...

Holy Crap!

We start talking dates that she can release, and what's available on the calendar and what might be best from a publishing perspective. We start with the 19th of January and work our way backwards when I mention I'm happy to help with her punch up, so long as she is ok with me *doing things* with her prose.

She assures me she isn't precious with her words and she sends me the manuscript and I have chapters 5-16 to do.

(There are a total of 19 chapters.)

I go ahead and start editing at chapter 1, because I need to refresh my memory with the story (I had read the beginning a few weeks back.)

It doesn't take too much time to get Chapters 1-4 done as she had already made a pass and I look in Slack and Joe (the Editor) is mentioning he is working on Chapters 1-4 and I raise my virtual hand and let him know I've got edits to said chapters...

I see I had a comment from Ellie about this.

Ellie's response to me editing 1-4?

Elllie: "Whaaaaa? I had first four PERFECT!!! :-0 !"

(Note the first instance of being a *little* precious.)

So, I end up editing to chapter 13 and send these chapters over to Joe the Editor (not exactly like Joe the plumber) the next day by noon my time. I finish the book later that night by 8:30 PM and Bob's your uncle.

Then, I have a conversation with Ellie about a few small tweaks I had made. In this case, a few 'Britishisms' that I took out and changed to the American word(s) and I find out I was sandbagged.

She absolutely is precious with a few words, *ESPECIALLY* with British words.

By the end of the conversation, I'm explaining I didn't take them ALL out, and I've no clue whether she is *truly* precious, or just giving me a hard time.

(I'm hoping she edits these author notes and clues me in, because I still haven't a clue.)

>> Ellie edit: I was just giving you a hard time ;) I'm not precious. As long as you don't change ALL my words.

Now, I tell you all of the above to say THIS:

When Ellie shipped over her story to give to me to punch up a little before Joe the Editor received it, she messaged:

Ellie: thank you so much for doing this... I hope you don't fuck it up ;-) #AuthorNotes

Ellie: it sounds funnier if we put a (beat) in between those two statements ^^^

... She has never told me if the first sentence is dry British humor, or the second sentence is an effort to help my ego and soften the reality that she hopes I don't fuck up the book.

(Truly, I'm thinking it is the former.)

Either way, *I sure hope I didn't fuck up the story!*

It felt GOOD reading Molly and the team again. For those reading The Kurtherian Gambit, I promise I've put in an Easter Egg about Sean in book 21 that you didn't know you were waiting for.

>> Ellie edit: Oh shit. Shouldn't we have talked about that... you know, so you don't fuck it up??

Ad Aeternitatem,

Michael

>> Ellie edit: wow. Only 1000 words? Someone is slipping... ;P

Ok, ... I've been encouraged for more words, don't ever say I don't step up to the challenge!

I'm presently looking out over the Sea of Cortez, with the Pacific Ocean off to the far right (I'm about maybe three hundred feet up in the air and a mile from the beach at most and I am watching two whales breach ... make that three, in Cabo San Lucas.)

The temperature is a very comfortable low 70's, but I am doing everything I can to hide in the shadows. I have no idea what it is, but that damned sun feels like a laser right now with any body part of mine that the sun shines on immediately feeling like it's 40 degrees hotter.

And starting to smoke.

It's a bit like heaven and hell, all on my balcony.

I started this extra snippet before my confab with Ellie. I'm finishing it after my latest confab with Ellie.

She says to tell you something something <It was funny, and I deserved the comment, but I really can't remember the details of the comment... It had to do with the fact that I was going to bring my pen out again for what reason? Because she dogged me about slipping? The answer is yes, yes I am.>

I spoke to her while she was in her new apartment in Austin, Tx.

It is apparently freezing for her there in Texas right now, while I'm worried about getting out of the sun. I decide not to make a big deal out of her situation because she is sick as a dog, coughing and sneezing with a head cold and in a town that is just balls cold.

I am thinking, "Wow, this is a *HORRIBLE* 'Welcome to Texas' moment."

However, in her indomitable fashion, she speaks to how the original instructions to getting to her apartment (which were waiting for her on the phone when she arrived) are convoluted, annoying and long. She's rolling her eyes thinking 'This is how I have to get to my apartment every time?'

Then, the next day she exits her front door, turns the other way, walks five steps to a door that drops her right off to the street outside.

You know, the one which is only about a block from her we-work space?

Good times!

Unfortunately, it also calls into question the smarts of the person who gave her the directions to her apartment in the first place…

Sigh.

I explain that everyone has a 'Cousin <insert name here>.' You know the one guy in your family (usually a guy) that is the one the News at 6 interviews when the flood waters are 5 feet high, and he is out walking in it the deep waters…

With an umbrella?

(Yes, that is a story borrowed from Jeff Foxworthy.)

However, Jeff is just speaking truth, which is why it is so funny. Apparently, Ellie received the directions to her apartment door from that cousin.

I hope Austin shows her why Google, Facebook, and so many start-ups and building their offices there.

Otherwise, she is going to be stuck thinking Austin is a city full of our cousins.

And while that would probably deliver untold amounts of funny author note comments, I don't wish that on even my worst enemies.

So, I'm off to continue writing TKG21 now, and then in the next couple of weeks working with Ellie on Michael's book 04.

Keep yourselves comfy in this horrible cold streak!

Ad Aeternitatem,

Michael

(*BOOYAH! 60% more wordage…*)

BOOKS BY ELL LEIGH CLARKE

The Ascension Myth
* With Michael Anderle *

Awakened (01)
Activated (02)
Called (03)
Sanctioned (04)
Rebirth (05)
Retribution (06)
Cloaked (07)
Bourne (08)
Committed (09)
Subversion (10)
Invasion (11)
Ascension (12)

Confessions of a Space Anthropologist
* With Michael Anderle *

Giles Kurns: Rogue Operator (1)

<u>Giles Kurns: Rogue Instigator (2)</u>

The Second Dark Ages
with Michael Anderle
Darkest Before The Dawn (3)
Dawn Arrives (4)
Deuces Wild
with Michael Anderle
Beyond The Frontiers (1)
Rampage (2)
Labyrinth (3)
Birthright (4)

CONNECT WITH THE AUTHORS

Receive updates from Oz by registering your holo/ email address here:
ellleighclarke.com

Facebook:
http://www.facebook.com/ellleighclarke/

Michael Anderle Social

Website:
http://kurtherianbooks.com/

Email List:
http://kurtherianbooks.com/email-list/

Facebook Here:
https://www.facebook.com/TheKurtherianGambitBooks/